Tetherbots

T. M. Rivera & Geoffrey A. Jourden

An Imprint of Fat Cat Talent, LLC

This book is a work of fiction produced by Fat Cat Talent, LLC. Any references to historical events, real people, or places are products of the authors' imaginations. Any resemblance to actual events, places, or persons, living or dead, is purely coincidental.

Fat Cat Talent is available for book signing at live events. For more information, email fatcattalent@gmail.com

Contents

Chapter 1 - Tit Jar 1

Chapter 2 - Foul Play..29

Chapter 3 - Murder in the Sex Spot................................ 45

Chapter 4 - Talking to Herself.. 49

Chapter 5 - Braylen..77

Chapter 6 - Too Close to Home 92

Chapter 7 - Make Money or Die Trying..................... 103

Chapter 8 - Killing Karen 111

Chapter 9 - The Precinct 116

Chapter 10 - The Hunt 126

Chapter 11 - The Aftermath 134

ACKNOWLEDGMENTS.. 137

Chapter 1
Tit Jar

Chenier Lynx Laurent's eyes rested on the Tech District of Neo Grid City, a paradox of a place overflowing with office warehouses, tech buildings, and ghostly remnants of demolished structures. Spooky Joshua trees and a long-forgotten mountain summit fringed the abandoned architectural remains in the periphery, touching the outskirts of Neo Grid City like sprawled-out, chalk outlines from an old crime scene. This was where the sex trade operated … the dead part, the Brothel District. The other half of the city was only alive because of the technology that kept its electricity running like an inferior vena cava, delivering oxygen-depleted blood back to the heart from the depths of its lower extremities. The Tech District held the lifeblood of the largest A.I. company in the city, Tetherbot. Its building was the tallest among the cityscape, an insane monstrosity climbing to one hundred and seventy floors, only a few blocks from Lynx's apartment.

With a view of the city from the living room of her one-bedroom apartment, Lynx cleared all her furniture to create the space needed for herself and her newly purchased Tetherbot to move around. Her apartment was located on the third floor in a converted bank, a high-rise in downtown Neo Grid in the Tech District. It was the most expensive city in the world to live in, but she managed to scrape by with an acceptable salary as a remote sales representative.

Lynx looked at her reflection in her cheval mirror, butt-naked aside from a tiny thong. She felt needlessly self-conscious, despite her five-six athletic frame and narrow hips—a great figure by anyone's standards. Body dysmorphia coupled with crippling anxiety wouldn't allow her to enjoy her tiny hips with ample thighs, full breasts, or little stomach pooch. In her opinion, her breasts could be one size bigger, her thighs could be two sizes smaller, and her little pooch could be a rock-hard six-pack.

Lynx opened her curtains, staring at the city moving both in front of and beneath her, busy with standard and flying vehicles alike. She opened her arms, praying someone would finally see her naked … exhilarated by the idea that someone would see all of her. For now, this was as close as she could ever get to the great outdoors. A *Blueship* taxi swooshed past her window, flying straight by like an afterthought. Then another. Lynx's heart drummed in her ears, accelerating faster and faster until it felt as if it was being squeezed by a snake. She cried out, cowering to the floor mid-sob. "Stupid ass, Lynx. I am DONE with this."

She wiped the tears with the back of her arm. "Anxiety? Do you hear me? I am talking to you. I can't live like this anymore. I *will* go outside, even if it's as a damn Tetherbot!" With that, she forced herself up and reached for her purse, where inside, an orange pill bottle awaited her. There was no name or prescription details on the bottle. It was MDMAX, a popular street mixture of MDMA and Xanax. With shaky hands, she opened the pill bottle and shook one magnificent pill out into the palm of her hand. She knew the rush of relief would come soon, like a best friend patting you on the shoulder, telling you, "Everything will be okay." Without hesitation, she popped it in her mouth and swallowed it dry, spinning around to look at the answer to all her problems.

Standing conspicuously in the middle of her living room was a big, black crate—approximately the size of a human being. Lynx opened it, revealing a piece of dainty paper, immediately reminding her of her favorite childhood story, *Alice's Adventures in Wonderland*.

Big box. Tiny paper. The words on the latter were an embellished Bold Artistic Serif font: *Welcome to Tetherbot. Together, VR Robot. Enjoy.* Inside were four important items: a lifelike, female robot, a shiny haptic suit (constructed to control the robot remotely), a stripper pole, and a pink, Bluetooth teledildonic device. Lynx knew once she put the headset on, she would not want to stop the sim, so she carefully constructed the stripper pole and set out the rest of the items, staring at them all in a line. Knowing what she was going to use these items for would have been enough to make her blush if Lynx felt things the same way normal people did. But her feelings were muted, as if she had been disconnected from the back of her head and put on a shelf to collect dust.

First, Lynx slipped her legs into the sleek haptic suit. She gasped lightly, shocked by the various sensations that were delivered to her body by over one hundred touch sensors. The new suit felt like silk, and she touched the grooves where the material surrounded the electrodes. Butterflies tingled inside Lynx's stomach followed by a slight arousal at the new polyester smell and thought of the suit's intended purpose. She connected the TetherLink feature to her headset, slipped it on her head, and began listening to the automatic, pop-up instructions.

Welcome to Tetherbot. The owner-operator assumes liability for their Tetherbot at the time of purchase. Never share your password with another user. Operating a Tetherbot to commit a crime is a serious felony, punishable under Federal law. Please use your Tetherbot responsibly. Before playing, please refer to your owner's manual for complete instructions. To link with your Tetherbot, double-click your palm and you will be taken to the home screen. There, you will be able to choose three options: simulation mode, automatic mode, and adventure mode. In adventure mode, your robot is free to roam. Any money you make or spend in adventure mode is attached to your TetherWallet. Before signing out, simply press the middle of your chest and your Tetherbot will return to its designated home address. We hope you enjoy your Tethering experience. Together, we are Tetherbot.

After the instructions were done, Lynx had the freedom to roam within the platform. It was all self-explanatory, operating like any other gaming system. Like most hardcore gamers, she ignored the *Tutorial,* which was for newbies who had never seen the platform applications. She was *not* a newbie, and neither was her best friend, Robert Chaise, who had brought over his Tetherbot, Orlando, as part of his college thesis paper for Neo Grid University. "I got to play with Orlando all night long," she had told Robert, who fell asleep on her couch that night, exhausted from his schoolwork. He awoke the next morning to see Lynx still playing in the sim. She had wanted a Tetherbot ever since that visit, saving for months to buy her own. Today, she could finally join the rest of the world.

"Okay, let's check you out," said Lynx. Double-clicking her palm, she selected simulation mode first. She felt the surge of the MDMAX working its way into her system as she expertly pressed the suit's sensors. Only moments earlier, her body had been a place of shame, seeking a permanent sanctuary. Now, with the increasing effect of MDMAX kicking in, her figure was methodically transformed into a beautiful temple—a God's feast revealed in a winter storm. Everything was beautiful, glowing, and alive ... including the lifelike robot standing across from her in her apartment.

Lynx waved her hand to the robot, and it waved back in perfect synchronicity. "Okay. *That* is creepy," she said.

"Okay. *That* is creepy," repeated the robot, at almost the same moment. Her voice was the same, imitating her with precise inflection, pitch, and tone. Lynx hated to hear her voice on a recording or see herself on camera, and this was no different. Lynx caught the glint in its eyes—the plastered smile that didn't quite contort to her exact dimensions. She didn't like that, but what was the alternative?

She looked at the robot apprehensively, stepping to one side. The robot moved to the same side of the room, copying her stride. Lynx knew it was foolish, but she tried to fake out the robot, turning around in a circle as fast as humanly possible. The robot turned around in a circle, matching her every move, a complete carbon copy. Feeling woozy and lightheaded, Lynx stopped and grabbed her knees, catching a glimpse of the robot in her peripheral. It was almost silly watching it imitate her dizziness. Once she got her bearings, Lynx jumped up and did a kick. Again, the robot copied her movements identically.

This seems easy enough. Now let's go outside for a stroll, Lynx thought. "What do you say? Want to go for a walk? Then get to work?" Lynx asked the robot.

"What do you say? Want to go for a walk? Then get to work?" the robot repeated.

Lynx smiled, thinking of the endless possibilities. She could finally do what she wanted to do, go where she wanted to go and make as much money as she wanted to make. Soon, her purchase could be put to work at the most elite cyber brothel in the country, and she could start making the big coin she was so desperately seeking. Tetherbot called their product The Zenith Experience. They called it this knowing how often their robots were used to do indecent things, according to societal judgment, such as what Lynx was planning … sex-tech perversion and exploitation. Other uses for A.I. robots included performing dangerous jobs, drug deals, and murders—though the latter happened sparingly since Tetherbot activities were always recorded. Some people got off on being watched and recorded, resulting in well-known daredevil streamers and influencers scattered throughout Neo Grid City. But most girls Lynx's age weren't interested in avatars or older men yet, especially older men with electronic fetishes, so it was important to stay safe. This was where the robot came into the picture.

Lynx wondered when her fascination with robots had started. She tried to think back to the last time she'd been touched in any way, whether it was physically, spiritually, or emotionally. A year of a dry spell at least. Perhaps she was suffering from a spiritual malady. That seemed to be the direction humanity was going. She pondered this new age, 2055, the age of the extending Aquarius—otherwise known as the age of enlightenment. Since 2020, Aquarius had gained momentum, and humanity had taken charge of its own destiny and its rightful heritage. These Great Months, or Ages, came with their own epochal stories of human change. This change had slowly shifted and taken a firm stance, festering in astrological constipation.

Oh, who was she kidding? Her problems didn't lie in the stars. This was about sex and money. Most girls her age were lost in the way of morals anyway, selling photos, sex, and experiences. What did it matter if she participated too? Lost in her own thoughts, Lynx performed a little practice dance, getting ready for her new job as a cyber brothel worker.

"Why a sex robot?" Robert had asked. "Why don't you get a real job using a Tetherbot?" The answer was simple … she had bills to pay, and fast. Tetherbots were cash cows and were becoming a more prevalent and necessary purchase to compete with the ruthless Epsilon Generation of today. Why not get paid to eat, breathe, shit, and masturbate like the rest of Neo Grid, cashing in on the Zenith Experience? "Anyway, who cares?" she told Robert. "The robot is having sex, not me."

Still lost in her thoughts, Lynx walked closer to the lifelike robot and touched her cheek. She gasped, startled by the unusual warmth of the robot's hand touching her in the same spot. Lynx quickly put her hand down to her side, turning her face to inspect the robot's details. She had fire-red hair, a small button nose, vivacious red lips, and perfectly set cheekbones. Her sparkling green eyes complimented her hair perfectly and were surrounded by purple and red hues of makeup. She was wearing a luxurious green dress with sheer black leggings and sapphire-studded necklaces around her neck. And her shiny green high heels matched her gown, rounding out her ensemble. Suddenly, Lynx wondered how this robot would pleasure anyone at all. She wanted to lick its face to check how it licked back, but maybe that was the pills talking.

"Who dressed you, a man?" she asked the robot, shaking her head. "You look like a green Disney princess threw up on you." Lynx took off the robot's shoes and tried them on. "Same size as me—just as advertised. It's your lucky day. You can use my shoes."

The robot was in the middle of repeating what she said with a slight delay as Lynx ran to her closet to retrieve a pair of clear heels she hardly wore. She never used any of them since she stayed home most days. The only time she ventured out was in the company of Robert, but his visits were few and far between. "Robert and robot … ironic," she had told him.

The robot ran after her, following at arm's length.

"What's this?" Lynx noticed a thin gold chain around the robot's neck and reached over, lifting it gently to read it.

"What's this?" the robot repeated, reaching over to touch Lynx's neck. The name *Sapphire* was etched into the necklace—the name imprinted on the outside of the textured black box she'd come in. "Sapphire. So that's your name. I love it already."

"Sapphire. So that's your name. I love it already," repeated Sapphire.

Lynx turned off Sapphire's simulation mode; she was used to being alone in the apartment. She had, in fact, lived alone since she was eighteen years old and had become used to solitude, as there were barely any visitors, not even so much as a family member … specially not family members.

Lynx changed Sapphire's shoes, inspecting her ensemble with her new and improved pumps. *Much better, but she still looks far too overdressed for a walk around here. Maybe I should take her out later tonight.* Lynx debated this before finally deciding to practice by walking the robot around the apartment and down the hallways of the housing complex.

*

It was two o'clock when Lynx set up the *Blueship* ride for that evening—pick-up at ten, destination the Cyberbar, a neo-zoom dweebie hotspot. Sapphire could make some connections and find out how to be initiated into the cyber brothel. Lynx had no criminal history to speak of, and the brothels were always looking for young girls to hire, especially because Cyberbrothel employees consisted of a lot of older women on their way out in life who decided to partake in the kinky side of the business. The brothels were places where anything went—drug deals, marriage ceremonies, cybersex, robotic toys, and orgies. They came in all different styles, from swanky high-profile businesses to dirty strip mall outlets. It was where the rich and the working class went to play and indulge in their deepest desires.

*

It was seven-thirty by the time Lynx stopped practicing walking around with Sapphire and recharged the headset. She microwaved her regular frozen dinner consisting of *Meaf,* a popular plant-based meat with flash-frozen vegetables and vegan gravy. After eating the last decent meal in her freezer, she showered and dressed in gray sweats, ready to take Sapphire out on the town. She limbered up with some yoga stretches and made sure to drink plenty of water first, then donned the headset and activated Adventure Mode through the TetherLink.

Zoom. Instantly, Lynx was looking out of Sapphire's eyes and moving her limbs and body. Lynx played around a bit, getting the feel before eventually making her way toward the door and heading for the flying *Blueship* sports vehicle waiting out front. It had chrome rims and the famous *Blueship* logo splashed across both sides.

As Sapphire approached the hovering *Blueship,* the door opened automatically. There was no visible driver, only three bright touch screens with control options. The car was fully automated—a driverless, hybrid taxi, capable of either land or air travel. These vehicles were commonplace, and most of the time, a safer alternative to operating a personal vehicle. Sapphire climbed in the passenger seat, and the door closed with a soft whoosh behind her.

The *Blueship* pulled away from the apartment complex, flying toward the bright city lights in the near distance. It passed all the city traffic and navigated into the old, abandoned ruins on the outskirts of the city, where the cyber brothels were located. As the hovering vehicle grew closer to its destination, it dipped lower, passing old buildings that were barely hanging on to life, riddled with broken doors and squatters. Graffiti decorated the front of the "for sale" signs, covering any trace of who you might call to purchase one. The media dubbed the misplaced humans living here, "Tetherless junkies," who couldn't assimilate into society. Sapphire settled back in her seat, using the touch screen in front of her to pick out music for the ride. Her favorite song, "Splitting Hairs," started playing as she danced along in her seat—her body rolling in full ecstasy after her full dose of MDMAX.

*

A couple of songs later, the *Blueship* pulled up to Cyberbar, which was lit in holographic lights and adorned with images of animated topless girls dancing above the signage. The *Blueship's* door opened, dinging, as an automatic robotic voice said in a monotone, "You've arrived at your destination. Thank you for choosing *Blueship*."

Sapphire carefully stepped out of the hovering vehicle before walking up six red-carpeted steps to the Cyberbar's front entrance. As the *Blueship* raced away, Sapphire greeted the bouncer standing in front of the door, trying her best to be heard over the loud music emanating from inside and the small group of people talking out front.

"Hey, how are you doing tonight?" said Sapphire.

"There's a cover charge of forty bucks, and I need to see some ID," said Carney. He crossed his muscled arms over his chest. His muscles gleamed beneath his tight-fitting shirt as he stood under the Cyberbar's neon lights. Lynx had met Carney when she'd first visited the Cyberbar, investigating whether there was real money to be made. Because of her irrational fears of going to places in person, Lynx had been heavily medicated at the time, and Carney, the bouncer, had noticed.

"No problem." Sapphire stepped toward Carney. He had a slim, shiny device about the size of a thermometer, holding it out in front of her eyes. Sapphire opened her right eye wide and stared into a light that turned on the scanning device's optical reader. A faint blue beam scanned her iris and beeped. *Transaction accepted. Identity authorized,* the device's screen read.

Carney looked down at it, then disabled the electrified barrier to give her access. "Right this way, VR girl," Carney said, waving her inside. Sapphire's face showed surprise, her mouth agape. "Yeah, I know it's you in there, Lynx. The scanner tells all."

"Oh, shucks. Just don't blow my cover, bouncer boy. Please?" She clasped her hands together, as if praying.

"Wouldn't dream of it," Carney said.

"Right," Sapphire said, turning a light shade of pink.

Sapphire walked inside and was immediately greeted by a waft of vaporized smoke clouds, causing slight moisture to glaze over her sensitive e-skin. Flickering lights hanging from the ceiling lit up the sizable dance floor, casting colorful shadows against an amber backlight from behind the bar. To Lynx, all the colors seemed to dance and shimmer as if mixed through a shiny, opaque face filter. The speakers blared out a familiar tune, as the crowd of club attendees gyrated to the beats. Sapphire walked over to the bar and was greeted by a handsome, golden-haired man with baby-blue eyes, sitting casually on a barstool. She thought he was cute, so she decided she wouldn't mind if he was her first client.

"Hey, a fancy-looking girl in this dingy establishment," said the man. His smile widened like a small white earthquake—or *was it earthcake?* She couldn't remember, as the drugs were taking their gradual hold of her. She would have to lower her MDMAX dose for the next go-round.

"Is this seat taken?" said Sapphire.

"Be my guest. But it's at your own risk," said the man.

"What is that supposed to mean?" said Sapphire. She plopped down in the seat next to him without hesitation, catching a large whiff of bourbon. Using Sapphire's sensors, Lynx registered his vitals, noting the signs that were consistent with intoxication.

"It means that every seat in the Brothel District is the hot seat, and you're sittin' in it, darlin'. There's a sadistic killer on the loose. But don't you worry," said the man. He turned on his stool, swaying a little bit in place. He used his free hand to steady himself, slurring. "Ol' Braylen is coming to the rescue."

"Who?" asked Sapphire.

"Me," said the man boastfully.

The bartender chimed in as she poured another drink. "You're not doing shit, Braylen—other than getting drunk and talking smack."

Braylen ignored the bartender, not taking his gaze off Sapphire. "Ignore Erin, for she knows not what I am capable of. So, have you been here before?"

"No, I'm new to the scene," said Sapphire. "Any advice for a newbie?"

"Don't go for your first John," said Braylen, looking around suspiciously.

"Why? Are you a John?" Sapphire smirked, placing her evening clutch purse on the bar directly in front of her.

"Heck no. I don't pay for sex. I have a free buffet pass in that department. And the name is Braylen. But you can call me Dempsey, my last name if you like."

Lynx noted the confirmation of his name and smiled. "No. You are the first of your kind, Braylen, so I'll remember," she said politely, beginning to scan the club for another potential customer.

"And you are?" Braylen eyed her observantly.

"Sapphire." She extended her hand, and Braylen accepted it graciously before shaking it vigorously. Her newly acquired nostrils picked out the smell of lavender baby lotion and a grape-scented hair gel. *Weird mix,* Lynx thought.

"Nice to meet you. So, you work here, Sapphire?" asked Braylen.

"No, not yet. Should I?"

"Depends." His expression sobered.

"Ooh, so mysterious. On what?"

"How much you like life." Braylen chugged his drink, setting it back down hard. He looked up at Sapphire as if she were a shiny new toy with complicated how-to directions.

Sapphire stopped smiling. "That's not funny."

"Yeah, and I'm not laughing. I'm only stating the facts," said Braylen. "The clubs in the Brothel District have taken the lives of two girls so far. Officials say there's a killer at large, targeting Tetherbots. You'd better get while the going is getting—if you know what I mean. Another one, Erin." Braylen raised his finger to the bartender.

Erin acknowledged Braylen and got to work on his drink, pouring a top-shelf whiskey, McEntire 28. She set it down and stuck her tongue out at Braylen. Erin was a young, peppy, top-heavy brunette with curly, shoulder-length hair, wearing a white shirt one size too small with printed red hearts over her nipples. Sapphire noticed partly hidden behind the bar, she was wearing a tight, black leather skirt, black fishnets, and leather boots.

"Then why do you come here?" asked Sapphire curiously.

"I'd offer you one, you know. What's your flavor?" Braylen said, ignoring the question.

"I prefer my own cocktail of confusion. Besides, I'd be well-advised to refuse from the sound of it."

"Yeah, if you're not careful, like these dim-witted, party-going fools. But I study the facts," he said loudly.

"What are the facts, and why do you study them?" Sapphire said, imagining how this conversation would go if one of them were sober.

"I'll tell you in one circumstance," said Braylen. He stared at Sapphire so brazenly that back at home, all of Lynx's insecurities seemed to swell to the surface like an orange dawn rising in the sky. It took her a second to recover, remembering that she was Sapphire.

"Which is?" Sapphire leaned in closer, detecting the woody, pecan tones of the whiskey on his breath.

"You can *help* me catch the serial killer," said Braylen, tensing his jaw.

"What? What are you talking about? Why would I do that … and why would you?"

"Because I'm a private investigator. That's my job," he said. He licked his lips, and Sapphire understood his insatiable desire was real and all-consuming. She noticed his nails, all bitten down to the quick. This was a man who lived, breathed, and shit work—then got trashed over it. She knew the kind. Lynx's dad had been one of those all-in types too, especially when it came to drinking. He had undiagnosed bipolar disorder with a heavy mouth and a heavy hand to match. A breath of trepidation tickled Lynx's brain as she recalled the pivotal night of overlapping arguments in the kitchen while watching T.V. Lynx had slowed her mind in caution at the time— scuttling and inching toward the kitchen door. In a drunken rage, her father had ripped off her mother's dress, yanking it clean off her shoulders. The next thing Lynx remembered was a pool of blood and the knife protruding from her father's neck.

Then the gurgling.

The gasping.

More blood.

When the cops arrived, Lynx's mom was naked and drenched in her dad's blood. While Mom was utterly embarrassed and humiliated, Lynx wasn't even sad that her dad had died. She was traumatized by the publicity of the news reports and completely mortified by the cops, who had seen her mother's naked blood-covered body. But sad? Never sad.

Lynx never dealt with the trauma but instead bottled it up with prescription pills and the bottle. But drinking alone, she had found, wasn't fun. It was an isolating thing that disturbed the demons inside of her.

"I don't like to talk to the law or anyone associated with it," said Sapphire, looking at herself in the bar mirror. Her puckered red lips popped in the light, and her breasts glimmered with an iridescent glow. She studied Braylen's reflection, noting the broad shoulders and camel-colored blazer. *What did this guy want?* She looked around the club, hoping someone else would catch her eye. She could make an excuse to bail now, but she would have to time it right.

"I'm not involved with the law. I run my own business and only work for select clients," said Braylen, interrupting Lynx's thoughts.

"Yeah? Well, I don't want to mingle with the likes of you. I came here to make money, not ruin my chances of it." Sapphire put one foot up on the barstool, getting ready to stand.

"Maybe we can be mutually beneficial," said Braylen.

"Oh? How's that, Mr. P.I.?"

"I can get you in with a high-profile clientele. All you need to do is be my eyes and ears," he said, his baby blues gleaming.

"Sounds like a lot of extra trouble for me. I could find my own way around."

"That would take a while, and it's more trouble than it's worth. You don't know all the players or who to avoid. I've asked all the hard questions around here. You wouldn't have to lift a finger," Braylen said with a cocky, smug attitude.

"And why should I help you?" With each passing moment, Lynx was becoming more uncomfortable.

"Because I see you. You don't really want to do this, but there is a reason why you're doing it. You need this." Braylen's eyes looked deep into hers as if he could see straight past the robot and into Lynx's soul. He grabbed Sapphire's arm.

"You don't know me." Sapphire pulled her arm away. "Stick to your P.I. work, not your phony attempt at psychoanalysis. Besides, I'll find someone else to help me for free. Now, if you'll excuse me … have a good night."

"Alright, alright." Braylen lifted his arms. "I get it. You don't know me. Here, take my number." He produced his WatchGo and tapped Sapphire's wrist, transmitting his data to her WatchGo.

"I won't be needing this. Oh, and Braylen? You owe me a buzz … because you ruined mine," Sapphire said.

"I'll be seeing you around," said Braylen. He smiled, watching her go.

"Not if I can help it," she said, waving him off.

Braylen's pink cheeks turned rosy red, and Sapphire caught one last glimpse of him looking dumbfounded as she casually strolled through the club toward the dance floor.

*

The club was alive with scantily dressed dancers on the LED flooring, its multiple colors transforming harmoniously with the different beats. Sapphire approached apprehensively but soon began to twist and turn to the sounds, entering the crowd like a fish swimming toward the fast-rushing rapids of a river. Lynx wouldn't have been able to get to the bar, let alone dance in front of people. But now she was Sapphire, goddess supreme, dancing for all to see.

"Hey, hey, yeah!" Sapphire sang along with the group as she flowed into the mix of dancers, finally landing face-to-face with a young, fresh-faced guy with brown hair, a sharp nose, and hazel eyes that she couldn't help but stare into.

"Hi, I'm Geir. Are you new here?" the stranger asked as he continued dancing.

"What? I can't hear you," shouted Sapphire.

"The name's Geir—pronounced like a gear," he said louder as he leaned toward her ear.

"Oh, okay." Sapphire laughed. "Sounds explosive."

"Yeah? How are you tonight?" he yelled.

"Better now that I have a dancing partner." Sapphire swayed to the beats.

"I'll show you my best moves." Geir put down his drink, stretching with a smile.

"Uh oh. Whatcha got? Let's see it then," said Sapphire, raising her arms.

Out of nowhere, the lanky young man improvised an entire dance sequence, shimmying his shoulders and tiptoeing, then shaking his booty with enthusiasm.

"Hell yeah. Let's do this," Sapphire squealed. She began gyrating and shaking, working her way closer to Geir. He grabbed the bottom of her waist, and she dropped backward—Geir scooping her back up again. He twirled her as easily as a feather, spinning her around the dance floor. Lynx felt amazing, exhilarated by the vertigo.

By this time, other patrons had noticed and gathered around to watch. Someone shouted, "Yeah, get it," as the couple twirled and twerked, gyrating, and whipping their hair back. Sapphire and Geir dipped low to the ground, and the crowd multiplied, buzzing with expectation. As they cheered, Lynx felt a surge in ecstasy, her lips involuntarily smiling as sweat dripped down Sapphire's face. She could almost taste the prescription-tainted sweat dripping into her mouth, and she twirled around some more, almost to the point of exhaustion.

"God, this is exhilarating," she yelled to Geir, who looked distracted by a particular onlooker. Sapphire followed Geir's gaze to a tall, dark, distinguished man, staring intensely at her. A waitress was talking to the onlooker, pointing over to the two of them dancing. She walked over to them quickly, tapping Geir on the shoulder and saying something in his ear.

Geir wasn't smiling anymore. He excused himself with an exaggerated bow, indicating the end of the dance. The crowd clapped, and Sapphire did the polite thing, bowing in return. "My lady, you can be my dancing partner anytime, but I must bid you adieu." Geir withdrew into the crowd, excusing himself the whole way.

"No. Don't go, Geir," said Sapphire. Some of the other partygoers tugged at him, urging him to dance again, but he went straight to the bar and ordered a drink.

The waitress turned to Sapphire, saying something that she didn't catch at first, and then placed something crisp in her hand. Sapphire looked down, astonished to see $1,000 cash wrapped in a currency strap indicating the amount.

"What is this for?" said Sapphire. Her forehead scrunched up as she scanned the room.

"The gentleman over there would like to pay you to leave your dancing partner so you can join him for a drink," said the waitress with a white, toothy smile. Her bosom was pushed up almost to her neck—the fluffy breasts and fake smile almost softened her words.

Sapphire scoffed, looking at the man from across the room, his dark eyes ablaze as he smiled at their conversation. What was he playing at?

"Follow me," said the waitress.

Sapphire followed the waitress hypnotically, telling herself this was an adventure. If she wanted to make money, she would have to go with the flow, unlike Lynx, who would run the other way. Besides, the man had paid cash up front.

The waitress led her to the mysterious man, who seemed to be dissecting Sapphire inch by inch as they approached him. He gave her a wicked smile, letting her know he had won this little game of "fetch the girl." Sapphire suspected the man was used to playing games and winning since he looked so thoroughly pleased with himself.

"Creative way to get me over here. You do that often?" said Sapphire, talking above the music.

"Only when it's deemed necessary. My name is Hazza Ebeid. And you are …?" The man had a voice like butter.

It was hard for Sapphire to concentrate on one feature of the man because like a puzzle, every piece was perfectly placed. His dark, penetrating eyes melted into hers as if he were watching a pleasant dream. Flawless olive skin and perfectly arched eyebrows lent him the distinguished appearance of royalty. His disconnected T-shaped tuft of hair accentuated his bottom-heavy lower lip. Back at her apartment, Lynx felt as if she had stopped breathing altogether, and her heart was fluttering in her chest. She wasn't sure exactly how old Hazza was, but she guessed he was in his mid-thirties.

"My name's Sapphire." Her voice felt a little small … as if it were shrinking before him.

"It's a pleasure to meet you, Sapphire. Shall we sit down?" Hazza stood and raised his arm to indicate the way.

"Sure," said Sapphire. *You are down for an adventure,* she reminded herself.

"Great," said Hazza, leading Sapphire to a quiet table booth tucked between two side stages.

"After you," he said, pulling out her chair. Sapphire sat down, and he joined her in the plush chair across from her.

"I hope you don't mind." Maintaining eye contact, Hazza pulled out an e-cigar and took a puff, blowing out two big O-rings of vaporized smoke in the air. A waitress came by and poured two shots of Battery Brand Bourbon, setting them down, side-by-side. She smiled and slipped past them as silently as she'd come. Sapphire smiled back, wondering if the waitress was a Tetherbot or a human.

The silence was deafening as Sapphire anxiously waited for someone to talk. Not being able to stand the silence anymore, she broke it first. "Why does everyone seem so afraid of you around here?" she asked.

"The boss is always the bad guy," said Hazza wistfully, scanning the club with a tired, distant expression.

"Oh? I didn't realize this was your place. How many clubs do you own?" asked Sapphire. She hoped Hazza wouldn't pick up on her age. She felt like an old soul, but was it enough to fool a successful business owner?

"About a dozen. We get all types of people here, as you can see. Here, you can be anyone you want. There is no racism, no sexism, and no limit to your imagination. Robots dancing with humans alike. You can't even tell the difference." Hazza pointed to the Tetherbots and humans intermingling.

"Impressive," said Sapphire. She didn't want to seem too eager, but she also needed to get down to business without sounding desperate. "But I was under the impression that one could find girls if one were so inclined. I don't see many girls dancing tonight."

"Girls … well, yes. As far as the eyes can see," said Hazza. He gestured toward the ceiling as if the possibilities were endless. "But you, Sapphire …" He paused, undressing every millimeter of her haptic-laced body. "Are a rare gem—a true beauty among plain stones."

"You really think so?" said Sapphire. She turned away, breaking eye contact.

Hazza laughed. "Oh, don't be shy. We both know how attractive you are."

"That's kind of you to say. But I've seen a lot of gorgeous girls trotting around here."

"They're beautiful for sure. But you … you're next level. You exude a 'je ne sais quoi,' if you will," said Hazza, winking.

This man was dizzying, intoxicating, and *oof*, she got a whiff of him when he moved closer to her. He smelled like chocolate, cigars, and expensive cologne. "Thank you," she said, blushing.

Hazza settled back into his chair, squinting. "You don't talk like a city girl. Where are you from originally?"

Sapphire began to speak, but Hazza interrupted, "Perhaps you are a suburban expat?"

"I was born right here—Neo Grid City," said Sapphire.

"Your parents ... they still live there?"

Deciding he wouldn't let it go unless she told him something substantial, Sapphire decided to be as blunt as possible. "Well, Dad had a wandering eye for something more youthful. In the end, he was out for himself, and Mom sort of lost it after that."

"Is she okay now?" asked Hazza, leaning in.

"No. But she's somewhere safe, considering everything that happened," said Sapphire, breaking eye contact. She focused on the patrons dancing, rather than on Hazza's hypnotic face. She felt a warm hand on her cheek, and then a soft thumb caressing her face. She was instantly soothed. *If I were a cat, I'd be purring by now*, Lynx thought.

"Dear Sapphire—so you lived alone afterward?" asked Hazza. His piercing stare spoke volumes, commanding the atmosphere around him.

Sapphire shifted in her chair, correcting her posture. If she was going to talk about this, she had to do it with an air of confidence. She wasn't used to anyone taking an interest in her (other than Robert). A smooth jazz song played in the background, helping lift the mood. "On my eighteenth birthday, that was my present to myself."

"Good for you. And you're happy now? Is that why you came as your T-bot?" said Hazza. Sapphire looked down at her hands, trying not to think of the game Hazza was playing—the one where the rich guy figured out everything about the girl only to lose interest. She had to prove useful, resourceful, and driven if she was going to keep his interest. Lynx thought of herself as a third person—someone who wasn't wanted or needed in the context of this conversation. *Why do I feel more normal as Sapphire than as Lynx? Lynx. I am Lynx.*

"It's that obvious?" she said. She imagined herself hiding in a gray rock, concealing her emotions from narcissistic prey.

"Well, you're beautiful beyond words, but there's something in the way you dance that tells me you can hold your own without your Tetherbot."

"I guess I could if I were the type to go out. But I'm a homebody, one could say. I feel no need to leave the comfort of my home unless it's absolutely necessary." *Now I sound like a domestic housecat. So much for adding value,* she thought.

"Oh, I never would have noticed. You seem so sociable." Hazza rested his hand close to hers on the table—his fingers almost touching hers.

"Yeah, well … I guess I needed this more than I knew," she said, blushing.

"I can show you things that you need … more than you know."

To this, Sapphire was quiet, her eyes widening. There was a pregnant pause, which she used to scan Hazza. Hazza sat with his legs apart, manspreading as if he knew he was on display. She noted his heart rate, steady and strong; he was not nervous in any way. He leaned in. "So, tell me, what brought you into my club tonight?" he asked, touching her arm.

Here was the trick. Hazza clearly liked her, but how could she possibly tell him she needed money without losing his respect? The best way to go about it was to approach it objectively.

"To tell you the truth, I'm in need of a new job, but … I'm inexperienced," she said.

"I see," said Hazza. He sat back in his seat, his fingers connecting.

"Do you?" said Sapphire, the words burning hot through Lynx. Suddenly, she felt embarrassed, as if she had crossed a line. "Listen, if it's too much, I understand. I can go somewhere else." She put her hands on her armrests, getting ready to stand.

"Please. Stay," said Hazza calmly. "I could use a girl like you, but I must warn you, there's a killer on the loose. He's already murdered two unlucky girls in my clubs, and who knows where he'll strike next." He took another drag from the e-cigar, chasing it with his bourbon.

"This is the serial killer that Braylen talked about?"

"So he told you and that still didn't scare you away," Hazza said, pointing his cigar in her direction.

"Of course, I am scared. But this is just my avatar. He can't kill the real me," said Sapphire.

"That's where you're wrong. This lunatic hunts down Tetherbots and their users alike. He's a twisted psycho who gets a rise out of torturing his victims."

"How do you know that it's a man? It could be a woman."

"You're right. It could be anyone. It could be you, for example," Hazza said. He took the extra shot of bourbon, handing it to Sapphire.

"I don't think so," she said. "I barely leave the house, as I've said." She grabbed the shot and set it down on the table, pushing it back in Hazza's direction.

"That being so, let me ask you this," he said. "Are you sure you'd be okay with this line of work? We have a wide range of customers, some of whom have very esoteric interests. You know, the kinky stuff. Imagine dealing with abnormal requests, plus dodging a killer."

Sapphire shrugged. "I know the risks. Yes, they are great, but the risks were just as great before this conversation. This is a dangerous line of work—selling sex. I've had time to consider it, and there is no other way for me to make what I need outside of this industry."

"That carries some weight," said Hazza gravely.

"I know," she said, touching his hand gently. "But trust me. I can handle it." Back at home, Lynx knew Sapphire could handle it. She could do the unthinkable. Suddenly, Lynx wished she *was* Sapphire, and an overwhelming desire to get rid of Lynx peaked in the forefront of her mind. *You don't need Lynx,* said a whisper, encircling and closing in on her. It came from a deep and dark place. After her parents had gone, Lynx felt like there was nothing left to hang on to. She had been left alone, like collateral damage.

"You could get hurt," said Hazza, touching her leg. Snapping out of her daze, Lynx was brought back to the present.

"Don't worry about me, Hazza. I can take care of myself. Besides, I always carry some protection." Sapphire pulled out a small silver laser knife the size of a lipstick case to prove her point.

Hazza chuckled. "That's cute, but you can put that away for now. I've beefed up security and added more surveillance cameras. We *will* stop this guy." He pressed his hands to his head, massaging his temples. Lynx noticed how quickly Hazza could turn from hot to cold. She imagined all the ways he must feel disconnected, stuck between juggling his business responsibilities with the weight of his sex workers' safety. Lynx visualized black body bags with polished red toenails poking out of the sides of a gurney.

"I'm sorry, Hazza," said Sapphire. She touched his arm to grab his attention. "But I still need a job if you'll have me. I've done the research, and as far as I know, there is no faster, more lucrative way to make money. In fact, it is more acceptable nowadays—as simple as eating or breathing, especially with an avatar."

Why was she acting so cavalier and so confident? She had agoraphobia, for Christ's sake! Then again, she was a curious, voyeuristic person, albeit online. She was informed—having watched videos featuring all sorts of fetishes. Fellatio, foot fetish, edging, cream pie, sadism, and the like—those were all terms she'd memorized in case anyone wanted to purchase them as extras. She had to take a risk, and Sapphire would take it for her. There was no better club for her, and Hazza knew it.

"Alright, then. How 'bout an audition? If you pass, we'll fill out the necessary paperwork, and you're in," Hazza said. He smiled and winked at her.

"What audition? What would you like me to do?" Sapphire crossed her legs.

"Well, I've seen you dance with your clothes on. But exotic dancing on stage in front of a crowd? That's a whole different skill set." Hazza smiled. Smoke billowed out from his nose, and he splashed another shot of Battery Brand bourbon down his throat. The more he drank, the redder his face turned. And the redder his face turned, the more boisterous his attitude became. He motioned toward a stage off to their left. An LED strip pole running up the middle was flashing blue, purple, and pink—the colors popping off it like an SOS beacon. "It's now or never. Let's see you up on this stage here. I'll get the DJ to get the music going, and we'll see what happens. What song do you want to dance to?" Hazza asked.

"'Kinships' by Splitting Hairs," said Sapphire.

"Alright, 'Kinships' it is. Be ready." Hazza sent a message to the DJ without blinking.

"Right here?" Sapphire looked around the club, turning in a circle.

"Yes. Here," said Hazza. He looked serious now ... expectant.

Lynx felt like she wasn't there—and technically, she wasn't. She realized after a few moments that she had never ventured this far out of herself—and she had never been so anxious. *Pushing yourself past your limits is a good thing. You never would have made it this far without Sapphire,* she told herself. With that thought in her mind, she walked onstage and slowly started peeling her clothes off. First came the dress, which was no problem, but hardly sexy, as it messed up her hair. She stiffened when it came off, aware of the cold breeze, then wondered where on earth to throw the dress.

This is a necessary madness, she thought. *There is nothing to fear here.*

She tossed the dress softly past her feet, then slowly started pulling down her leggings. They got caught up at her thighs, and she looked over at Hazza, who was sitting with his legs wide open and his lips parting in a relaxed state. Sapphire slowly let her leggings fall to the floor and kicked them toward Hazza. He caught them and looked them over—then looked at her again with one eyebrow tweaked up. "Naughty girl. Is that all you've got?"

Exposed with nothing but a G-string and lace bra, Sapphire grabbed the pole with one arm high, sticking her butt out. She touched her stomach alluringly all the way down with her other hand and grabbed the bar at a lower part, hoisting her body up the pole slowly but surely.

Hazza hollered toward the crowd on the dance floor and waved a group of loyal patrons over to the side of the stage. "Come over here and get a look at the new blood! She's got some moves!" He grinned with pride as more and more people gathered around the stage. Most of them were waving twenty-dollar bills around.

As Sapphire inched her way along the pole toward the ceiling, Lynx found herself surprised at how easy it was to lift her own body weight. Lynx was using the pole at her apartment. She was athletic, but hoisting her whole body up the entire pole would have taken all her core strength, rendering her breathless. But no one could see Lynx's flaws in the sim world. Sapphire performed effortlessly, without sweating, without panting, perfectly showing off her assets. She dropped to the floor, performing the splits, and the crowd roared in response. Anyone who had doubted her before this move, would assume she studied pole dancing before. Still, she wanted to make this dance look natural, so she tried to give it the most unstudied appearance she could.

Once on the floor, Sapphire got in front of the pole and laid down, lifting her legs in the air to shake them back and forth, twisting and thrashing her booty vigorously in the process. She knew she had to slow the dance down, so she began to grind steadily, gradually climbing back up the pole. This time, when she reached the middle, she twirled slowly, her hair flying around her in a red fiery circle. Opening and closing her legs slowly, she teased and taunted her audience. As she looked at all the mesmerized faces in the club, Sapphire knew she had won the crowd.

*

By the end of the night, Lynx had a job, and Hazza was thoroughly impressed with her, showing her off to his friends and asking her engaging questions. His entourage asked questions, too, such as, "How did you learn to dance like that?" "Are you single?" "How much for a private party?" Finally, Hazza asked, "Now, why do you need a job again?"

Although she felt it wasn't anybody's business, she offered generic responses, which seemed to appease them. Overall, she was pleased with herself. With all the money she'd made tonight, she could buy a better wardrobe and ultimately make a lot more money. Although she was fond of saving and paying for essentials, she could already afford to start the emergency psych fund she needed for her mom. No more white knuckling it or worrying about her future. With this gig, Lynx could save, uproot, and work from virtually anywhere. Satisfied with this conclusion, she told Hazza it was time to retire for the night.

"How will you be getting home?" Hazza asked.

"I'll take a *Blueship*," Sapphire said firmly.

"Nonsense, I will take you," said Hazza, touching her arm.

"No, I can't. Not tonight." It was too much stimulus. She needed time to process ... somewhere quiet to be alone.

*

Sapphire watched as the *Blueship* disappeared, wondering what Hazza's true motives were. She walked up the dirty, concrete steps toward her apartment building, still thinking about the things that had transpired during the night. It was pitch-black outside, with only one light on each floor to guide the way; the rest were burned out, posing a safety issue. The faded red brick facade with green vinyl siding looked uninviting in the low light, but it was home.

As Sapphire made her way up the apartment steps, she heard a faint voice from the shadows under the stairs. "You're in danger. Don't trust anyone."

A chill ran down her spine. Not wanting to look back, Sapphire bolted up the two remaining flights, heading straight to her apartment, as if through muscle memory. She fumbled at the door, feeling the presence of someone still behind her. Rushing inside, she slammed the door and secured the lock, inadvertently dropping her purse and all its contents, including all the cash tips she had made. In her peripheral vision, she saw Lynx standing there. It was like a severance from self ... a surreal out-of-body experience, seeing herself through Sapphire's eyes. Part of Lynx didn't want to go back to her body, even though she'd never left. That part of her felt like she could be Sapphire forever.

Chapter 2
Foul Play

The following day, Lynx was working her boring sales representative job, staring at her computer screen, when the numbers began to blur on the spreadsheet laid out before her. She couldn't focus on the task at hand. Her mind was preoccupied—haunted and unsettled by the creepy voice that she'd heard the night before. The words, *You're in danger. Don't trust anyone,* repeated over and over in her head, even in her dreams.

Who was it? Who are they warning me about? Lynx was already wary of a few of the new characters she'd met the night before. And while she'd been scared when she was Sapphire … today, as Lynx, she was truly terrified. The amalgam of physical and emotional pain was severe and almost too much to bear, including fear, nausea, paranoia, dizziness, and headache.

Lynx wondered what was causing all the side effects. The MDMAX? Possible, but unlikely. She took it all the time. *What could it be?* At one point, the media had aired a piece about adverse reactions after prolonged use of a Tetherbot, including hallucinations, dizziness, headaches, and psychotic breaks—but they were rare. And she had only used her Tetherbot twice. Yet here she was, head pounding, dizzy, and nauseous. She slowly ate some crackers and chased them down with lukewarm ginger ale to calm the symptoms. The help was fleeting and only moments later, she barfed the entire contents of her stomach into a wastepaper basket, not even having time enough to make it to the bathroom.

I better get some of these accounts settled before my boss gets on my ass. After looking at the time, Lynx was typing in the last few numbers on the TPS reports when her boss's face appeared on the screen, filling the entire surface of her computer in a red light.

Damn, just what I didn't need, Lynx thought. She tried to protest or ask for more time, when a prerecorded message spoke: "Ms. Laurent, this is Mr. Steele. If you're receiving this message, you have been terminated, effective immediately. Your final paycheck will be transferred to you in five to seven business days. Thank you for your service, and good luck to you in your future endeavors."

"Well, fuck you too, you son-of-a-bitch!" Lynx shouted at the screen. The program shut off automatically and logged her out, transferring her over to a customer service site.

"What the hell did I ever do?!" Lynx said, slamming her computer shut. As abrupt as it might have seemed, she knew her tardy reports and lack of attendance at meetings had been the culprit. In this economy, it didn't take much to fire an employee over the slightest misstep; someone was always ready to take your place.

Lynx shouted into her WatchGo, "Call Robert!"

The watch trilled and Robert picked up the call on the third ring. His face lit up on her watch, all smiles—his warm reassuring face reminding her of better times. "Hey, you. What's up? Long time, no talk … stranger."

"Stranger? Says the guy who was missing in action for how long? Are you still with that same girl? What's her name again?" Lynx popped a piece of gum in her mouth, chewing vigorously.

"Vannoy? Nah, she's ancient history," said Robert.

"Oof, sorry. Are you okay?"

"Pssh, yeah. Of course," said Robert. "These girls are interchangeable these days. Nothing a little adventure won't solve."

"Yeah, I feel that. Speaking of adventures … you remember how I wanted to buy a Tetherbot," Lynx said.

"Yeah, I think you mentioned it. Whatever came of that?"

"Well, I got her," said Lynx, beaming in a sing-song tune. She dashed a couple of steps and sat next to Sapphire, putting her on the screen. She hugged Sapphire and smiled at Robert. "See her? Isn't she a beaut?"

He whistled before speaking. "She looks so real. I would never have known she was a Tetherbot," said Robert, looking at Sapphire with a critical eye.

"Yeah, I played as her last night, and it was amazing. I got a job the same day, then got canned from my real job just now."

"Wait, what? Why?" asked Robert, munching on a tortilla chip.

"I don't know. Because I *suck* as a real person?" she said angrily. She stood up and got a step stool, then began to rummage through her entire medicine cabinet to see what was there.

"Uhh, okay," said Robert. "First of all, don't do anything stupid."

"And second of all?"

"Don't do anything stupid," he laughed. "But for real … just stop it, Lynx. I know how you get. Are you sure this other job is safe? Where are you working?"

"I'm at the Cyberbar," said Lynx, suddenly imagining herself as Sapphire again. She felt a rush as she found her extra stash of MDMAX and popped half a pill, praying it would stay down.

"Lynx Laurent! Do you know what I heard about that place? My buddies say, 'Don't go to the brothel district … a crazy person is killing the workers.' Dudes don't want to die with their junk out for display. And taking pills to boot, Lynx? It's dangerous."

"I don't have a choice. I have bills to pay. You know about my mom."

"Is she still in the Amethyst Ward?" Robert asked. His eyes expressed concern.

"Yes, she's still there, probably for the rest of her life. They've got her so spaced out with drugs, she's like a zombie. And every time they try to taper her off, well … it's for the best that she stays there." Lynx was surprised by the sound of her trembling voice.

"Have you talked to her recently?"

"No, and I'd like to keep it that way. I have to work and make some money first."

"And what about *you,* Lynx? This is a lot to handle. Work like this is damaging to the soul. You don't want to end up self-medicating more than you already do."

"It's not *me* performing the work. It's Sapphire … and she doesn't have a soul," said Lynx. She chose to ignore the medication comment in the spirit of maintaining a good friendship.

"At least make sure both you and your Tetherbot have protection," said Robert. His eleven o'clock frown lines squeezed inwardly, furrowing at his brows.

"Protection? Sapphire can't get pregnant," Lynx said, laughing.

"That's not what I mean, and you know it. Have you considered buying a weapon?"

"Yeah, sure," Lynx fumbled in her purse, producing a laser knife. "I've got this."

"I don't like it. I think you should just go back to another online sales job. Just because the last one didn't work out doesn't mean you can't find something better. Just my opinion, but you're not right for this work. When do you go back again?"

"Tonight," said Lynx, bracing herself for Robert's response.

"*Tonight?*" shouted Robert. "Do you have a death wish? Listen to me. Make sure you have protection and ping me Sapphire's location when you get there. Deal? And if you ever need a spot on one of your adventures, give me a ring. Just like old times."

"Like the time we got addicted to that video game. *Slasher City …* remember?" Lynx said, then smiling. She grabbed her remote and flipped through her TV, looking at all the games she owned. It was an ungodly amount—over four hundred and sixty. She hadn't even realized her gaming addiction had been that out of hand. In her defense, that was the number one source of entertainment for most of the citizens living in Neo Grid City.

"How could I forget? You schooled all of us that night," said Robert. He looked at his WatchGo, with his brow furrowed. "Alright, I've got to go to work. But I'll see you later. Call me anytime you need. I mean it. I worry about you."

"I worry about you, too," said Lynx, smiling before she hung up. She grabbed the VR headset from her dresser and unplugged it from the charger. Then she carefully examined Sapphire to see if she needed any grooming. Lynx was getting wet in her lacy black panties just thinking about going out as her alter ego.

What should I wear tonight? I need something sexy, she thought. She walked into her small but cozy bedroom and rummaged through her clothing. She had hidden all her sexy clothes in her customized LED nightstand, although she had no idea who she was hiding them from. Probably herself since she never felt perfect enough to wear them. Judging from the current queue, she would have to improve her lingerie. The thought of wearing sexy clothes as Sapphire was slightly arousing. After perusing her nightstand, Lynx was pleased to find a handful of entertaining ensembles in her collection.

"Oh, Sapphire. You're going to look good tonight, aren't you," Lynx spoke conversationally, carrying a collection of clothes in her arms and laying them out on her bed. Sapphire had a little smudge of lipstick on her face, but it wiped away effortlessly as Lynx washed her face. "Time to sync up and share thoughts," she said, speaking in the same tone she would use to tell a dog to sit.

Lynx put the VR headset on. This was it. There was no going back, and no one else to depend on. It was only ten-thirty in the morning, but she was eager to use Sapphire. She could spend the whole day inside Sapphire's body for all she cared, side effects be damned!

Lynx turned on the headset and the familiar Tetherbot jingle played, instantly firing Sapphire to life. Using her body to control Sapphire, Lynx made the Tetherbot get up from the couch and head out the door. She spoke into her WatchGo and ordered a *Blueship* pick-up to drop her at the Cyberbar. Lynx hoped Hazza wouldn't mind if she started off with a day shift. She didn't think he would mind for two reasons. One—once you were hired as a cybersex worker, you were a contractor, calling your own hours; and two— Hazza probably wouldn't be there at this hour ... none of the important men would be. She also hoped Braylen, the buzzkill, wouldn't be there sharing his ominous, fatalistic views about the world like a wet blanket ready to smother her. She didn't need him to tell her the world was bad ... she already knew that. Braylen was bad for business.

*

The *Blueship* dropped Sapphire off at the front entrance of the Cyberbar at eleven in the morning ... opening time. She looked around the building cautiously before stepping out of the vehicle. Nothing was strange or out of the ordinary: there were two junkies sitting on the sidewalk talking to each other with a grocery cart full of cans, old blankets, and clothing. The club looked closed at first glance until a beefed-up bouncer opened the double doors for the day. It was Carney, who seemed distracted by a large cup of coffee. He let Sapphire walk right in, and she made a beeline for the girls' dressing room, not bothering to look around or talk to anybody. She pulled out a chair and sat down facing a large mirror that spanned the entire side of the room. She glanced at herself with a smile, adjusting her tits and tugging her little black cocktail dress down.

Turning to her right, she noticed two other girls sitting further down. They were changing clothes and getting ready for their first show of the day. Sapphire noticed one of the girls had a Bluetooth electric cum-milking machine—she guessed it was for a customer. It appeared to be a large, two-handed operation, which was both intimidating and clunky. Is this what sex came down to ... putting an electric appliance on your crotch only to sit back and do nothing in return for anyone? Sapphire laughed at the thought and put her duffle bag on the counter and glanced around the room.

"Oh, hi. I'm new here," said Sapphire, trying to direct her eyes to the girls and not the machine.

"Yeah, we saw your audition last night," one of the girls said, and Lynx took a moment to admire her brown skin and DD bust. "You had some really nice moves. My name is Naomi, and this is Candis." She motioned to the girl with the milking machine. "You're Sapphire, right? We're here to make money and make fantasies come true." Naomi chortled. She was on the shorter side, standing at 5'1," but that only further accentuated her bubble butt and twenty-three-inch waist. Even though both girls were gorgeous, Naomi was the classic beauty out of the two, with her golden-brown hair cascading down past her breasts.

"Yeah, dirty old men's fantasies," Candis retorted. She laughed too, her shiny blue lips accentuating her white teeth. Sapphire imagined her as a shiny disco ball under some black lights. Everything on her was shiny and ultramodern, from her pink and blonde bobbed haircut to her blue vinyl S&M corset.

"No, that's who *you* keep attracting because you want the easy money. She's got daddy issues," Naomi said, directing her attention back to Sapphire.

"Well, well, well. So, you took the job anyways … decided to stay at the Death Club," said a familiar voice from the doorway. Sapphire spotted Braylen; his golden locks were stifled in a hat and paired with a monochromatic camel-brown color pantsuit. He waltzed in like a dandelion in springtime.

"Oh, get the fuck out of here, you damn pervert! We're half naked in here, Braylen!" Naomi shouted.

"Yeah, like I haven't seen all that before," said Braylen, standing at the door examining the room. He seemed less interested in the girls than the general space itself, as if he were looking for clues.

"That's not the point," Candis said. "We have privacy in here, and out there are the paying customers, you cheap-ass loser."

"Whoa, whoa, whoa," Braylen said smoothly. "The insults keep coming. I think you need to show some respect to the man who might save your ungrateful ass from a serial killer."

"You couldn't save your dick from your own pants if they were on fire," Naomi said, smiling.

"Good one," Candis said, giving her a high five.

"Yeah, yeah, yeah. Keep up the laughs. You'll be needing me one day. Then who's gonna' laugh? The killer, that's who." Braylen turned to leave, but then stopped and looked right at Sapphire. "I thought you were smarter than this, kid. I warned you about this place. It's no good. You'll end up dead. Don't trust anyone." Braylen tipped his hat and then walked out briskly.

"Hey, wait! What did you say?" Sapphire shouted to no avail, as Braylen was quickly out of sight. The way he said, *don't trust anyone,* sounded exactly like the voice from the previous night. Had Braylen been stalking her?

Sapphire turned around, mouth gaping and eyes wide in shock. Naomi walked over, putting her arm on Sapphire's. "Oh Sapphire, lighten up. You realize that man is a dumpster fire, right? Everywhere he goes, destruction follows. The poor guy can't help it … he's cursed. I wouldn't be surprised if he was the killer at this point. You know, a copycat fanatic. Probably needs the job, the poor loser."

"I don't know," said Sapphire. "I just got here, but it's like someone doesn't want me to be here, Braylen included."

"Oh, don't let him get you down, honey," said Candis. "He wants what he can't have, and that's these." She pushed up her tits, smiling.

"Slut," said Naomi. She pushed Candis lightly, and Naomi laughed.

"I just wish I knew what was going on," said Sapphire, fidgeting with her hair. "Anything that would help me not get killed, so I can make some real money. I need this job, you know?"

"We all do. Look," said Candis. "We know the killer is real … we can't deny that. But he's targeting *all* the clubs, not just this one. And we aren't going to let him stop our bread and butter—not when we can stick together and stay safe. Right, Naomi?"

"It's worked so far," said Naomi. She grabbed her purse, tucking it under her arm. "And our customers don't seem to mind the peep show. Like sometimes I watch, or Candis watches, and other times, our customers watch us. No one's the wiser. In fact, we learn things about each other we never knew before." She smiled, as if she was remembering something funny.

"Right," Candis said. "And we don't spook the customers by mentioning the killer, because there's no other way to make money this fast."

"Exactly," said Naomi. She continued talking, but Sapphire zoned out.

Back at home, the thought of these women dying concerned

Lynx—but she thought because of her own checkered past, she had no choice. Her mind spontaneously wandered back to the last conversation she had with her mom. "That *thing* you call your father is not a man. He was an inhumane creature, not worthy of sharing blood with you. He didn't deserve you. And now you don't want a relationship with your homicidal, suicidal mother … I get it—raise crows to have your eyes plucked out. Just know, if you have the same blood as your father, it's narcissistic blood through and through. He ruined us all, you included. In the end, we will all bleed—all die as a family for what we have done to each other. He threw the first stone. Remember that. This is your burden to carry now. Your stone … your legacy."

"Sapphire? Hello? Did you hear me?" said Naomi, waving her hand.

"Uh … yeah … sure," Lynx snapped herself out of her memories and motioned with Sapphire's hand. "Let's get out there and make that money."

"No, you weren't even listening," Naomi said. "I said it's slow in the daytime. You'll be lucky to make a decent amount of money, but we have some regulars who like threesomes and orgies, if you're interested. They come during the day to cheat on their wives, mostly."

"What does it entail?" Sapphire bit her lip, chewing on it.

"Oh, the usual," Naomi said. "We grab a couple of our guys, and we're off to the VIP room for some private time. It's fun. The guys get a kick out of it, so it's lucrative." Naomi ended with a wink.

"It's about time to hit the runway. Let's take our clients for an afternoon fuck fest," said Candis. She laughed as she headed out of the dressing room toward the stage, dressed in purple lingerie and clear high heels.

"Fine, I'll be right behind you. Just grabbing my shoes," Naomi shouted as Candis quickly walked away. She put on her eight-inch red LED-illuminated ankle boots, zipping up both sides. "C'mon, Sapphire. We don't want to keep our Johns waiting. Follow my lead."

Sapphire followed Naomi out of the dressing room and onto the main dance floor, where two handsome men were smiling, waiting with shots in hand. The men looked at Naomi with a happy expression, no doubt remembering all the intimate moments they've shared.

"C'mon, hussies. We haven't got all day," said Candis impatiently. Candis seemed codependent on her colleagues, Sapphire noted. Lynx reminded herself of her recent job loss, (only an hour and a half ago according to the VR headset) and forced herself to focus. She took note of one of the men, who had light brown hair and beady brown eyes. His wide smile reminded Lynx of a local T.V. anchor's smile. The smile didn't seem to match the beady eyes, but still, he was handsome in a Clark Kent kind of way, even if his intelligent expression looked as if it was masked by some unknown character flaw. From the first assessment, Lynx guessed he was a politician.

Beady Eyes' buddy, by contrast, was dashingly handsome, resembling a stalky, modern Superman, complete with broad shoulders, dark hair, and piercing blue eyes. Sapphire's fake heart began to thump loudly … an added feature in all the new Tetherbots.

As they approached the table, Superman handed Naomi and Sapphire shots. Sapphire couldn't stop herself from asking, "What's this?"

"It's a melon ball," said Candis. "This hunk offering you a shot," she touched Superman on his buff shoulder. "His name is Cannon because he's built like one." Although he was built like a brick and taller still, Candis' stripper heels made up for the difference, rendering her only a couple of inches shorter. "And this handsome man is Merit," Candis touched the beady-eyed man on the arm and smiled adoringly.

"A gentleman and a scholar," said Naomi, grabbing her shot.

"Not in the bedroom," Merit moved his hair out of his eyes and smiled.

"Then let's go to the VIP room, where there's more privacy," whispered Naomi.

"After our shots," said Cannon. "Today, I need to get inebriated."

"Cannon is an expert in business law. He's a tax attorney," said Naomi dotingly.

"I help the girls get their maximum tax deductions, since sex toys are a business expense," said Cannon, generating a laugh from the group.

"Let's drink to that," said Sapphire, meeting Cannon's shot glass with a clink, then downing it in unison.

"That hit the spot," said Merit, putting down his shot glass on the table.

Through Sapphire, Lynx experienced the alcohol's intoxicating effects, registering the data and simulating a drunken state that filled her haptic sensors with euphoric transmitters that flooded Lynx's senses with dopamine.

"Wow," said Sapphire breathlessly. Without hesitation, she downed the second shot before anyone else could.

"Atta' girl. That's our cue, boys. Cheers," said Candis, holding her glass out high.

"Cheers," they said together, clinking their glasses and chugging their shots.

"Whoo! I am feeling that already," said Naomi.

"Really? Show me," said Cannon, flagging a waitress. Using the Cyberbar App on his WatchGo, he repeated his last purchase. He added the VIP Experience to his cart with one click, reserving a large room with copious amounts of champagne.

The waitress hurried about her business, coming back to retrieve the group, "Follow me. My name is Rubix," she said. She led the way, embossed in a two-toned geometrical neon green bodysuit and shiny purple lipstick. It was so mesmerizing that Sapphire hardly noticed her purple hologram stiletto boots, which didn't match the bodysuit.

Sapphire turned her attention back to the men. Cannon walked between Naomi and Candis with an arm wrapped around each girl. "Yeah, we work hard; we play hard too. But we'll be able to retire early," he said.

"Ooh, can I retire with you?" asked Candis.

"If you're a good girl," said Cannon.

"Yeah, so be good for goodness' sake, Candis," said Naomi, teasingly.

At this, Cannon grabbed a handful of Naomi's right buttock, then slapped it with his big paw of a hand. Sapphire guessed Naomi was his favorite of the two girls, perhaps due to her cheeky responses. Naomi was intelligent and beautiful, and Sapphire couldn't help but watch her butt swagger as she took each step.

She noticed Merit taking the time to hang back, walking slowly beside her. "So how are you feeling, Sapphire?" he asked. He appeared to be a man of great observational skill, carefully watching her facial expressions, posture, and eye movement.

"I'm feeling good," said Sapphire, smiling.

"No, I mean about all this. It's your first time, right," said Merit.

"I mean, I view it as a transaction. I'm not used to intimate physical connections in any capacity, so this will be different for me."

"Maybe you'll enjoy yourself?" said Merit.

"Perhaps. I guess we will see," said Sapphire.

"Well, let me know. If you do like it, maybe I can see you more often?" he said.

She thought about that. "Yeah, maybe. Let's find out afterwards, shall we," said Sapphire, making strong eye contact to capture the full effect of this statement. As Sapphire's eyes locked with Merit's, she felt a strong burning in her loins.

Merit grabbed Sapphire's hand, giving it a little squeeze. She smiled awkwardly.

Not having had the opportunity to meet many people after her childhood trauma, Lynx became nervous for Sapphire and realized this sexual work adventure was not quotidian, despite the technology of the age. Sapphire hoped her customers, like Merit, also possessed the ability to hold a decent conversation, or she wouldn't get far. Attraction was not always dependent on physical appearances. She would grant her customers time to get acquainted with her, just as she had given her psychiatrist more than one session to get to know her. In her experience, people don't always blossom and open up at the first meeting, so she shouldn't expect much out of today.

At the flick of the waitress's wrist, an automatic sliding door opened, leading to a large, swanky room filled with light music. To the left was a beautiful, brown leather bed with red accent pillows. A mirror hung above the bed so a person could watch the room. The room was extravagant, more than what Sapphire had originally thought the club could afford and had large red satin curtains draped around the bed and windows. Dim candles lit up the right-hand side of the room, leading to a loveseat, a big recliner, a round coffee table, and eventually, the massive bar, which was arrayed in a semi-circular fashion. The waitress motioned them inside.

"After you madams," said Cannon with an air of chivalry. The three women walked in, followed by both men.

"Have fun," said the waitress, waltzing away as the door slid shut again.

"This is gorgeous," Sapphire said in awe.

"Right? I told you she'd love it," said Candis to Naomi.

"She'll love it better once I get my hands on her," said Naomi.

"Hey, me first," said Candis, dancing her lingerie off and throwing it to the side.

"See? Didn't I tell you we have fun," said Cannon, loosening his red tie. He took it off carefully, setting it on the coffee table.

"There's champagne if you need it," said Merit to Sapphire.

"Actually, I'm good," said Sapphire, removing her dress slowly. Merit stared at her in awe, his eyes sparkling. Cannon took the time to enjoy the view, too.

Naomi bounced from foot to foot, fanning herself as she observed Sapphire. "Damn, you are hot, Sapphire. Hew weee." She giggled, helping the men out of their suits.

Everything was going so fast, flooding Sapphire's senses. Back in her apartment, Lynx's heart was drumming in her chest as Cannon threw Sapphire on the bed with her back arched. She was suddenly surrounded by both men and both women. Her undergarments were removed and thrown off so fast that she couldn't tell whose hands undressed her.

Everyone thrashed about the bed, limbs entwining. Shoulders met shoulders, tongues met tongues, genitals met genitals. There was throaty laughter, followed by giggles, and Sapphire heard Cannon say, "Show me," to Naomi again.

Merit was paying special attention to Sapphire, licking, and kissing her all over, firmly pulling her closer as he penetrated her. His gaze was drawn to her lips as they panted, heads tipping back in ecstasy. Sapphire felt hotter and wetter as the time passed by ... and then suddenly it had been an hour and a half. Lynx was transfixed, overwhelmed by the orgy, forgetting any of her fears. It was a sublime bonding experience, with Sapphire and Lynx joining as one. It wasn't until each grip grew more intense, each thrusting grew faster, that Lynx realized they were getting closer to the end of their adventure.

Cannon exploded with a loud moan.

"Hence the name, Cannon," said Naomi, laughing.

Merit climaxed a few minutes later and was still throbbing when Candis licked the juices up.

Lynx shivered from a tingling pleasure she had never experienced in her whole life. This job was the stuff fantasies were made of, and somehow, she felt unworthy of this dream.

Back at home, Lynx realized she was dripping cum down her leg, hot and bothered and utterly alone with no one to love on. There was a deep disconnect between Sapphire's life and her own reality. She felt like a goldfish, looking through a small bowl. The world was so big, so full of experiences, all of which she was missing out on. In a short span of time, she experienced a rainbow of emotions—joy, jealousy, anxiety, pleasure, and fear.

She ripped off her headset and pushed the home button, sending Sapphire home alone in automatic mode. She gave her the courtesy of calling her a *Blueship*, but for the rest of the night, she didn't want to see that damn robot.

Chapter 3
Murder in the Sex Spot

"Baby" Blue Ryder was one of the hottest new girls at The Cyberbar, fresh off the boat from Finland. At least that was the backstory her model was given, according to her VR user, Kathy. Kathy was a sixty-three-year-old grandma-next-door type who lived vicariously through her VR vixen. She was having the time of her life in retirement and experiencing all the sexual activities she'd missed in her youth. Her seasoned experience made for desirable conversations and delectable afternoon delights, equating to some serious buck for her bang.

It was a typical Saturday for Blue as she arrived at work. She made her arrangements, texting her client as she dressed. She waited for the hot romp with her high-roller client in the VIP room—champagne and caviar ready. Red leather couches lined the walls, with a small red heart-shaped bed in the middle of the room. The shaggy red carpet added the final touch to what felt like a Valentine's Day clearance sale. Blue lay on the bed, wearing a black-laced bra with straps attached to her black-laced panties, garters, and black leggings. She was sipping on the champagne, slowly eating a cracker with caviar, as her camera recorded her every move for her thousands of online subscribers. Her gentleman was late, so she was taking requests from her viewers. They loved watching her eat and drink as she performed sexual activities. No one knew she was a Tetherbot, and she had no desire to expose it, so eating and drinking helped solidify the reality in her mind.

What is taking him so long? she thought. *He's usually punctual.*

At last, the door buzzed. Blue looked at the video feed to verify who was at the door. Her customer was dressed casually in a button-up bowling shirt and cargo shorts, like a tourist in Vegas. He investigated the small, mounted camera, smiled, and waved.

"He's here. Are you ready for some hot, sexy action, my friends? Tune in live," Blue said, as she opened the front door with a press of a button.

The door slid open, and a dark figure walked in, looking nothing like her friendly Vegas companion, Michael, from the previous video feed. Blue was confused and failed to put two and two together yet. The mysterious masked man was dressed in all black, with dark shadows following him.

"Michael? Is that you? You look like you're attending a masquerade party, dear. Come closer—out of the shadows where we can see you. We're here, live."

The shadowy man wore a long black trench coat over a gray button-up shirt. He was in plain black pants with white stains, topped off with a black, fedora hat. As he stepped forward and bent towards the light, his face came into view, and Blue gasped. Before she could scream, a three-foot-long needle pierced her neck, and a jolt of electrical energy zapped her systems. The man stayed slightly in the camera's peripheral view, only exposing his arms and one side of his body and hat, while his face remained hidden from the observer's view. "Baby" Blue was paralyzed, the needle steadily zapping her circuits.

"You see ... fellow viewers ... "Baby" Blue is but a puppet. A phony … only a Tetherbot." The man's creepy voice was made even more horrifying by a voice modifier, altering the sound frequency.

The message board was buzzing with comments about the unfolding scene, mainly about the revelations of Blue's identity.

Xtragold: *Blue is a God damn synthetic. She deserves what she gets!*

Anabanana: *What? I had a suspicion.*

Hollysings: *Blue lied. She was asked whether she was a synth or human months ago. She swore up and down she was real.*

Deathstinger: *Does it really matter? She's beautiful and robots are people, too.*

StikkenMoov: *Yeah, it matters. If I want to watch a Tetherbot, I'd fuck my toys at home.*

Ladylunatiktok: *Is this even real? Looks fake.*

The messages kept coming as the killer slid the needle all the way through Baby Blue's neck. The needle was extremely sharp and thin, seemingly shrinking as the masked man moved closer to his victim. His devil facemask was now in full view of the camera. A classic devil face, goat horns, and an elongated chin, adorned with metal spikes around the eyes and forehead filled the screen.

"Blue Ryder must pay for her deceit … not just her robotic body, but her living self, lying in her bed at home … Kathy is paying the ultimate price as we speak." The devil man lifted his gloved hand and pointed his finger in the shape of a gun at Blue.

"Bam … bam," he said as he gestured a shooting motion. The needle in "Baby" Blue's neck surged with a visible blue hue. Her previously blue eyes turned red with blood splatter, and her blonde hair started smoking at the roots. Blood oozed from her nose, eyes, and mouth, dripping down her face.

At home, Kathy was experiencing a similar fate. She was paralyzed in what looked like a trance, her VR headset strapped to her head, and her arms firmly clenching the bed sheets. Her teeth were tightly clenched together, grinding away in a grand mal seizure. Blood dripped from her mouth where she'd bitten down on her tongue; Kathy couldn't move, but she could still see what was happening to Blue.

The masked man looked at her, staring deeply into the camera as if he could see Kathy's face. Then he pulled out a razor-sharp surgical blade and brought it up into Kathy's view. She couldn't scream, she couldn't move, all she could do was watch as the blade moved closer and closer to Blue's eye until the tip of the blade penetrated the soft tissue and dug its way into the orbital circuits, popping and sizzling as the electronics were severed and mangled. With precision and swiftness, he removed the eye and held it out for all to see, artificial blood dangling on the wires as he waved it around. Finally, he stopped and waved it in front of Blue's remaining eye.

"You see this? Your treachery will not go unpunished. You will die from the technology that you used to deceive others." The masked man crushed the eyeball in his hand and dropped it onto the heart-shaped bed.

The needle was still through Blue's neck as the devil man took out an odd-looking gadget from his pocket. It was shaped like a skull and crossbones and about the size of a silver dollar. He stuck it to her forehead, and it clamped on with tiny micro-hooks. The skull's eyes lit up green as it hummed at a low electrical frequency. Blue's head swelled up like a balloon and the back expanded and cracked like an egg as fluids and wires shot out from the cracks until there was only a pile of wires and fluids on the bed. Blue's body collapsed on the bed, and the devil man retrieved the needle from her neck.

"Blue is dead," the killer said. "And back at home, Kathy is a brain-dead, an old bag of flesh. By the time anyone finds her corpse, her cats will have eaten what's left. A fitting end to a deceitful hag." The killer looked directly into the camera, unblinking bloodshot eyes staring into oblivion. And the feed went black.

Chapter 4

Talking to Herself

The next day, Lynx was surprised to see a large sum of money transferred into her bank account via her TetherWallet, the most popular cash app in Neo Grid City. She felt bad and hoped the group could understand why she'd left prematurely. However, given the ten grand sitting plush in her bank account, she had visions of a future walking around in plain view, living a good life … the life she was living through Sapphire.

Lynx sat next to Sapphire on the loveseat, determined to have an ordinary conversation. Maybe it wasn't normal to talk to a robot, but Lynx was beginning to think that Sapphire was the key to her therapy. For the first time in years, she'd thought about going outside to feel the warm sun soaking into her skin. What she had learned from other agoraphobics was to never give up: you never know which combination of therapy will work.

She turned to face Sapphire with a watery gaze, smoothing out her oversized nightgown. "Listen, I know I shouldn't have made you go home alone with a serial killer on the loose. For that, I'm sorry. But it's not fair that you get to have all the fun without me. Think about my point of view. I've been stuck living in this dinky apartment, working my ass off to pay Mom's medical bills. And you?

You just waltz on in like it's no big deal, making a cool ten grand on the very first day? You've made my life irrelevant. But you're also helping me in some strange way. I want to go outside like you, make money like you, have fun like you … but mostly, I wish I was you. You see, I feel more myself when I'm you than when I'm me. Does that make sense?" Lynx stared at Sapphire, whose makeup had faded after the previous night's sexual escapades.

"I guess I should be glad it's you and not me. I've never been in an orgy, so you can see how overwhelming that was," Lynx went on. "Don't get me wrong, I was aroused, but I didn't use the dildonic, and that left me hot and bothered by the end of the night." She spoke awkwardly, fidgeting with Sapphire's hair. "I know what you're thinking … I should have used it, but it was my first time sleeping with a stranger, much less strangers. I've only dated *one* guy my entire, pathetic life, and he was such a disappointment in the sex department. Not the kind of winner you'd want to lose your virginity to," Lynx paused. "I could have used your help back then, to be honest. I made bad choices when left to my own devices."

Lynx waited a moment as if expecting an answer, but the robot just sat in silence. "You don't understand. I was young, ruled by hormones. I still am, I guess, but staying at home helps me. I'm afraid to go back out there and try new things after what happened. After my narcissistic dad left Mom … I mean, before she killed him, I hoped a relationship would save me. But Dillon didn't care about me. No … just like *Daddy* didn't. And do you know the worst part? Dillon got someone else pregnant straight away, the same way Dad did. Dad had a baby with the nanny, you know? The fucking nanny. What kind of animalistic human being impregnates the help? Haha, you tell me who with all your fucking data." Lynx laughed dryly thinking about how unfunny the situation really was. "Don't you have something tucked away in all your programming that will fucking fix me? A solution to help deranged people like me, you know, someone who talks to robots?"

Sapphire, vacant eyed and in rest mode, stared off in the general direction of the fridge.

"No? Then I guess I have to do everything myself. Make the money for Mom's psych hospital ... like it's my fault she went postal." Lynx stood up and sighed, walking into the kitchen. She opened the fridge and grabbed a bottle of water, chugging the whole thing. By the time she'd finished the water and closed the fridge, Lynx heard a large thump behind her. Startled, Lynx dropped her empty water bottle and turned around to see what the heavy thud was.

Sapphire was lying on the floor, sprawled out, her hair disheveled.

Lynx rushed over, crouching down. "Oh shit! Are you alright?" Lynx picked up Sapphire and hugged her. "I'm sorry I'm so crazy. I didn't mean to go off like that. Thank you for everything. We will make some money tonight, and I promise to let more of me shine through you. How does that sound?" Lynx stared at Sapphire, then patted her head. "Okay, let's get back to work, then."

Lynx lifted Sapphire and took her to the bathroom, undressing her carefully. It seemed smart to bathe the both of them at once, so Lynx undressed and drew a bath, adding her most luxurious bath soap. Lynx sat in the warm lathery water with Sapphire, feeling the night's tensions subside. She gently cleaned Sapphire, washing her breasts, her thighs, her stomach, and finally, her vagina. Lynx's pussy pulsated, her nipples hardening and standing at attention. Suddenly a disturbing realization hit her: she had an irresistible urge to have sex with Sapphire. Everyone else got to, so why couldn't she? Maybe she would feel more connected to Sapphire if she did. Like masturbating. It was a form of self-love and self-care, wasn't it? It sounded like a good idea.

After entertaining the idea for over half an hour in the bathtub,

Lynx realized she *would* have sex with Sapphire if she could. And while it might be an empty, one-sided emotional exchange—in a way, it would be like making love to herself. Lynx wondered if Tetherbot sex required too much effort for a moment of awkward passion. Was she an odd anomaly for not wanting to deal with real people? Then again, it was not so strange in this day and age … was it?

Lynx ran it through her mind once more, *Sapphire can have sex with the customers, and I can have sex with Sapphire.* She stood up, then sat back down, plopping back in the water. "You really are a temptress, aren't you?" she said, using a cup to wash the bubbles off in a hurry. Enough was enough; she refused to rationalize her perverted line of thinking. With that, Lynx shelved her desires, consciously putting them away for another time.

She got up, stepped out of the bathtub, and dried herself off, then Sapphire. Getting dressed, Lynx recognized the sad fact … she never had anyone to get ready in the mornings with … never had anyone or anything to care for, not even a pet. In some sad or sick way, Sapphire was becoming her confidante and best friend. Without lingering on that fact, Lynx took a nap, hugging Sapphire and feeling safer than ever.

*

Sapphire finally made her way to work in her usual choice of transportation, the *Blueship.* Lynx made sure she and Sapphire had enough to eat for the entire day since it was Friday, Cyberbar's busiest night. There was no need to push it, Lynx decided, especially after the large chunk of change she had made yesterday. From what she understood, strippers and cybersex workers became used to a plush, freelancer schedule. She only hoped she didn't get too used to it, or else it would be tough to assimilate back into the white-collared real world. Or what if *this* was the real world—as real as it was ever going to get. She looked out of the window at all the expensive, flying cars in the sky. This inflated life took big money. The more she thought about it, the more she realized it was the kind of money her old job could never provide. What if Sapphire's sex work could help Lynx retire? Plenty of women worked for the clubs into a ripe, old age with the help of their ageless avatars.

Sapphire walked into the Cyberbar, where two rent-a-cops stood their ground, double-checking customers' driver's licenses directly inside the door. "Listen here," the shorter, bald cop shouted. "You wanna' stay in the club? We've got to notate your ID and frisk you. Move forward or turn around and go back where you came from."

A few of the patrons in line muttered and turned around to leave, while the others who chose to stay took off their shoes and waited to be frisked. After being deemed clean, they grabbed their belongings. Sapphire made her way through the crowd, barely escaping Braylen, who was boisterously describing the killer's possible motives to the other patrons.

Sapphire was equally surprised to see at least thirty customers already on the dance floor, grinding away to the rave music, unfettered by the extra security detail. Mind-altering music, much like the mysterious Arabian Riff is to the king cobra, played at a high volume, entrancing the dancers. It was spellbinding for the high-end customers, who were transported into their little worlds of wonder with whichever female companion had tickled their fancy. But above the musical elements came loud snippets of Braylen's tale, disturbing the peaceful trance. So far, the patrons seemed to be ignoring him as they continued twisting and writhing to the music.

Sapphire walked past all the action into the dressing room, where she was greeted by whiffs of cheap musky perfumes and sweet body lotions. She was surprised to catch a glimpse of an older woman in her early fifties, all gussied up with signature stripper hair extensions, fake eyelashes, and red lipstick. Her shoes had seen better days—they were scuffed up at the bottom and stained with wine and bodily fluids. Lynx couldn't understand why a woman of her age would choose to stick with her own physical form rather than a Tetherbot. Did she not fear the serial killer—or was she simply overly confident? Surely, she didn't make as much money with her wrinkles out on display. It was a bit like leaving laundry hanging out to dry, given all the technology and medical advances at hand. Then again, Lynx supposed there might be a few customers with a fetish for older ladies. Given what else people seemed to be into, it certainly wasn't the oddest idea. But what were the reasons for looking so imperfect, especially when rubbing elbows with Barbie look-alikes? It didn't matter … Sapphire would mind her own business. She had her own clients to find, and apparently, orgies to avoid. While she enjoyed the sex the other night, Lynx thought she was one orgy away from PTSD or a nervous breakdown.

Sapphire spotted Naomi and Candis, so she hurried over, putting a bag of fresh clothes in a locker for later use. Today was going to be her first full day building her own clientele, and she wanted to ensure her social skills were on point. If they weren't, Lynx planned to take more drugs to compensate.

Sapphire was about to close her locker when one of the bustier, Japanese-style Tetherbots with green eyes and red hair approached, her enormous boobs preceding her. "Hey Sapphire, the DJ wants you to check in. Share your favorite tunes with him. Cool?"

"Sure, anytime. What's your name?" said Sapphire.

"Oksana. Nice to meet you," she said in a thick accent. Oksana fidgeted with the silky straps of her dress, which kept falling off her delicate shoulders.

"That's beautiful. Russian? I detect an accent," said Sapphire.

"Yes, born and bred. At least, the real me." Oksana smiled.

"How long have you worked here, if you don't mind me asking?" Oksana seemed shy, and Sapphire wondered if she was possibly a loner like herself.

"Oh, I've been here for about a year now," said Oksana. "A veteran in stripper years. We don't last long, even less with the killer roaming the city."

"Yes, I heard. Did you know any of the girls?"

"I knew 'Baby' Blue. She was like a mother to us; kind of like the house mom that does all of our makeup. She was older, so it was a big shock when the killer chose her. It scared us. If he can kill her, he'll kill anyone. No one is safe." Oksana shook her head.

"That's terrible. I'm sorry about your loss."

"Yeah, we are like family here, so we took it hard. Just watch your back, and if you can work with others, do it. You don't know which day will be your last," said Oksana.

Sapphire didn't think she should press the questions much further. "So, about that. I don't know how well I handle group dates, but maybe if I work on busy days, I'll be good. Which days or nights are the busiest?"

"You're looking at it. By Friday, people are ready to get their party on, especially the ones with hybrid or remote schedules. They need a change of pace." Oksana bent over to fix her right heel strap with half of her breasts slipping out of her dress. She popped back up in a whirl, her black hair pinwheeling behind her. Her revitalized locks released subtle hints of cigar smoke, ylang-ylang, patchouli, and bergamot. The tropical, earthy aroma was extremely alluring.

"Thanks for your help," was all Sapphire could awkwardly manage.

"No problem. Good luck," said Oksana. She walked away, leaving the perfume lingering in the air for a few seconds after.

Sapphire speculated that the killer could be anyone … Hazza, Braylen, the man who had followed her home, a pissed-off customer, or one of the workers posing as a Tetherbot. She walked over to the DJ booth in a blur. Introductions were made. DJ Car Mell was wearing a brown hoodie with baggy jeans and had light brown skin and a short afro. He introduced her to some tunes she might like, but after a while, she was overcome by the thought that he too could be the killer. She picked out some sultry, sexy songs and a few techno beats before hastily making her way out of the booth.

As the next song finished, DJ Car Mell interceded. "Okay, ladies and gentlemen. Up next on center stage, is a fresh face. Please give a warm welcome to the new girl on the block … Sapphire."

Sapphire started dancing slowly to the music, as she spotted a plump, overweight guy sitting in the front row. He was wearing a tight, brown suit with pinstripes, and a pair of brown, Velcro, senior mobility shoes. His enormous belly hung over his belt buckle and food-stained matching slacks.

As Sapphire danced near the side of the stage, Naomi grabbed her and pulled her low. "That's Stan Milkford," Naomi whispered. "He's a regular customer, known for spoiling the girls he fancies … sometimes cash upfront if you can stand him."

"Thanks," said Sapphire. She walked seductively up the stairs to the pole in the middle of the center stage. Backing up against the pole, she pulled up her leg in a side split, caressing her leg slowly from her calf to her inner thigh, right next to her thong. Effortlessly, She hoisted herself up the pole, performing a complicated Allegra Oversplit that she had learned at home, holding herself up with one leg while lifting the other up in a side air splits. Lynx had done her homework after the orgy, and she was determined to be taken seriously when onstage. With some difficulty, she flipped upside down, splitting her legs in the air in a move called the Bird of

Paradise. By the time she slipped back down the pole into the splits, several customers were already lined up around the stage to tip her up close and personal. She smiled, walking over sensuously to her customers. She attended the white-collared men first, knowing these were businessmen on the go, who didn't want to wait.

Shoving her face to the floor, Sapphire hoisted her butt up and in the customer's faces, dramatically grinding up and down. She twisted up and flipped on her back, pulling her legs up in the air to gyrate, pulsating each butt cheek. She inched her way closer to the horny customers, who held out their money eagerly. Two customers grabbed her G-string, gently slipping money into it. The money came slowly, but steadily, much to Lynx's pleasure.

Once the first couple of twenties were in her G-string, Lynx got the itch for more. More was her problem, after all. She smiled as if she'd won the lottery, tearing off her top and throwing it into the crowd of thirsty men. It was then that an influx of money rained down on top of her—so much money she could smell it. She looked up, trying to decipher where the money was coming from, but there were so many dollar bills floating down, she could hardly see. Determined to find out who the millionaire rainmaker was, Sapphire twisted her way back up the stripper pole. That's when she saw the fat man, stomach bulging over the second floor railing with a suitcase full of cash, casually tossing its contents at her.

Sapphire finished the the rest of the song while riding the pole, laughing at all the money ribboning and slipping past her. When the song was over, several girls had to grab buckets to help Sapphire scoop up all the money from the stage and dance floor.

DJ Car Mell interjected: "Alright. Sit back and relax folks, because it looks like it's going to take a clean-up crew to help Sapphire out. You can slip to the second or third stage for some more side action, and I'll play some of your classic favorites while you wait. Next up on the main stage is Candis."

Candis gave a thumbs up to Sapphire as she walked toward the main stage. "Great job. You got Stan's attention. Now you should go talk to him." Candis waved her hands away from herself in a repetitive motion, shooing Sapphire away toward Stan.

"You go," said Sapphire, secretly eyeing Stan in her peripheral view.

"I can't. I've tried. He doesn't like me," said Candis. "Trust me. It's more money than you'll make for months on end."

"No way. That guy with the velcro shoes," said Sapphire.

"Not kidding. All his ex-girlfriends are set for life," she said without even a hint of sarcasm. "The girls you don't see working here. It's because of *him*." Candis looked up wistfully.

"Fine, I'll give him a try," said Sapphire. She grabbed her clothes and put them on as quickly as she took them off, leaving her shirt in the crowd.

"You got this," said Candis, smiling. "Everyone loves you, especially my customers. Merit says hi, by the way," she added with a wink.

Sapphire's mind instantly wrapped around a fresh memory, a sudden flashback of Merit on top of her, penetrating her as deep as he could. Rather than responding properly, she smiled sheepishly, never looking into his eyes. Lynx thought about her father. Morbid reflection told her she would not be in this club securing transactional sex, had he treated her better. Should it feel this normal for men to use her and treat her like a sex object? Was she overcompensating by picking this shocking career path in a pathetic attempt for attention? Or did she have a Daddy complex?

As Sapphire walked up the stairs, Lynx thought about how much she missed her father. She remembered the good times, like the time he taught her how to shoot a basketball, or the times he'd gone to her track meets. But things at home seemed to quickly deteriorate after she entered junior high. By the time she was in her teens, all she remembered was her parents fighting—the word "cheater," escaping her mom's lips on more than one occasion. By junior year, her dad's drinking became so frequent, there was hardly ever a sober moment in his life. Slowly but surely, his reckless behaviors and infidelities started to eat away at Mom until finally … Sapphire shuddered. Without realizing it, she found herself standing in front of Stan, staring at a yellow mustard stain on his bulging belly.

"Heya, gorgeous," said Stan, snapping Sapphire out of her daze. He spoke with a Southern drawl, which immediately got her attention. Not many people in Neo Grid City spoke with an old school Southern accent.

"Hello. How are you?" said Sapphire, forcing a smile.

"Doin' good, darlin'. How 'bout yourself? Enjoying yourself out there?" Stan smiled broadly, exposing a little lump of spitless, smokeless tobacco in the form of a snus bag on the bottom right corner of his mouth.

"I do," said Sapphire, curtly. "I enjoy dancing, I mean."

"Well, you look mighty fine doin' it, too. What's your name?" Stan's blue eyes were penetrating—his only attractive feature.

"Sapphire." Sapphire reached out her hand to shake his, and he took it firmly, giving it two and three pumps with a strong grip, never breaking eye contact. Sapphire felt slightly uncomfortable with the exchange, knowing that a man of this type sought to dominate. At least, that was her first impression.

"It's nice to meet you, Sapphire. Would you like to accompany me for a drink … or perhaps dinner if you're hungry?"

Of course, he was hungry. Stan looked like a pink-flushed Butterball turkey. But he had a boyish quality to his fat face that wasn't completely objectionable. Perhaps one could get used to it, especially if one liked fat-faced animals, such as pigs, groundhogs, or chipmunks.

"I'll take a drink," said Sapphire quickly. She would have to warm up to this man, so maybe drinks were what she really needed.

"Alright, let's sit somewhere more private," said Stan, smiling. "I've already prepaid for you to skip dancin' for the rest of the night and tipped you a handsome sum for your time in advance. Anything else we come up with is purely extra. No strings."

Lynx wondered if the kind of people who said, "No strings attached," really meant that *more* strings were attached. Like untrustworthy people saying, "I'm a good guy," or "Trust me."

Cautiously, Sapphire let Stan lead her to a small, but stylish VIP lounge area on the other side of the upstairs bar. As they entered, they were greeted by a waitress in a bright blue dress, who motioned for them to sit down on a plush couch that was facing the door. "Hey Stan," said the waitress, unveiling a huge, red-lipped smile.

As she took in her surroundings, Sapphire wondered what sum of money a handsome amount to Stan was. One thousand? *Ten thousand?*

"Well, hello to you too, Linnea," said Stan, warmly. Sapphire had to give it to the Southerners—they always seemed so friendly.

"Would you like your usual—the Mad Hatter?" asked Linnea.

"Sure, and whatever my lady-friend Sapphire wants, too." Stan's belly bopped up and down, spilling over his pants as he spoke and waddled around the room.

Sapphire noted the mustard stain again and analyzed Stan's appearance. *The signs of a rich man are seen in his belly. The heftier the man, the larger his wallet.*

"And what can I get you?" Linnea looked at Sapphire warmly and genuinely.

Sapphire was grateful to feel welcomed by her. This woman could be a good ally, leading her to more rich men in the VIP area. "I'll take a glass of wine, please." She put her hands between her legs, feeling a slight chill. She guessed it was her nerves acting up again.

"Well, alright then." Stan smiled. "So, how are you doing tonight, Sapphire?"

"I'm good. Getting acclimatized—second day, and all," Sapphire said, touching her hair.

"Yes, I've heard about you here and there."

"You have?" Sapphire was taken aback. She wasn't sure if this was a good thing or a bad thing, especially due to the nature of her business. What could Stan have possibly learned about her in two short nights?

"Most of the girls are flat-out jealous, of course," Stan said. "They're sayin' you're the best dancer they have ever seen. Some are saying they wish you'd teach 'em."

"*Me?* Teach *them*? How come they haven't asked me?" Sapphire was flattered. Even though she was an introvert, she was intrigued by the idea of making friends through common interests, or perhaps, common enemies.

"I guess they are intimidated—as pretty and talented of a dancer as you are. Where did you learn how to dance like that?" Stan adjusted his belt, tucking in his shirt.

By this time, Linnea had made her way back, and she was quietly setting the drinks down.

"I taught myself," Sapphire shrugged. "I guess being at home alone, one gets bored."

"You never have to be bored again. Not now that we're friends." Stan lifted his glass, tipping his head.

"Thank you," said Sapphire. Slowly, she was warming up to Stan.

Stan raised his glass for a toast, "Cheers to all the poor people in the world. I wonder what they're doin'."

Sapphire smiled, comparing her old life to this new one. She thought that maybe, if she latched on to Stan, her days of struggling could be long behind her. Could rubbing shoulders with the rich rub off and stick? Could she hold her own in this new world, earning value solely on companionship? Sapphire lifted her glass, "To the poor and unfortunate. May we find ways to add value to their lives."

Stan clinked his glass with Sapphire's. "Well said. You're an old soul, Sapphire. Pray tell, where are you from? Tell me a little more about you." He took a big gulp of his Mad Hatter.

"I'm from Neo Grid City, born and raised. There's not much to tell. I kept to myself and lived on my own as soon as I turned of age. Not to be plain vanilla. I suppose people expect a long answer, but I'm a blank slate … fresh canvas, so to speak."

"Well, that's just lovely, darlin.' There's a lot to be said for a capable, independent woman such as yourself. You don't see many these days. A lot of these fresh faces want an easy buck, thinking a smile and some masturbation can earn 'em some money. They don't want to work, much less dance. I don't know why they think we want to come in, if not for the touch. If I wanted to watch porn at home, I'd do that. But I'm a hands-on kind of guy."

Sapphire smelled Stan's breath as he spoke—it was a mixture of dip and gin with a hint of hamburger and onions and there was a little crumb in his beard stubble. She drank her wine faster, wondering if she should excuse herself so Lynx could take another hit of MDMAX. Instead, she thought it more prudent to change the subject. "So, what line of work are you in, if you don't mind me asking?"

"Don't mind at all," said Stan, sipping his drink. "I was the sausage king of Neo Grid City. I started out persevering in the greasy-grimy fast-food industry but have since branched out into real estate and casinos. I own SpiritZ Casinos. Have you heard of it?"

"Nope. Can't say that I have."

"Never gamble?"

"Not if I can help it," said Sapphire. *As if I need another addiction,* she thought.

"Smart girl." Stan chuckled. "But you'd be surprised how lucrative sports gambling can be. Of course, there's always blackjack, craps, roulette, and slots. I'll show you sometime, if you're interested."

"Sure, but I'm kind of a homebody." Sapphire shifted in her seat.

"We'll have to change that. Ain't no fun in that, is there?"

"You're not having fun right now?" Sapphire teased. She was forcing herself to flirt, seeing no other way to push this along to make some real money.

"Oh no, ma'am," said Stan, reallocating his big body closer to Sapphire. "I'm havin' a ton of fun. The way I see it, we can have a friendship long and true, so long as you're comfortable. Are you comfortable with a friendship, Sapphire?" His tone of voice was both sleazy and endearing. Sapphire supposed this was the way older men flirted. And she guessed he was about to get down to brass tacks, explaining what he wanted and for how much.

"Sure, I think I'd like that," said Sapphire.

"Well, alright. I'll give you $20,000 a week to start. Let's say we go to the 'red room' … get to know each other a little better?"

"Alright." Sapphire drummed her feet on the floor, foolishly excited at the prospect of big money. She blinked less, trying to pay attention rather than show how much the money strummed at her heart.

"Good, because I've booked the private room already," said Stan, picking up his phone.

Sapphire stared at Stan, noticing his socks, which were brown and mousey. She wondered if they smelled bad. She also wondered what his toenails looked like, because if they looked anything like his teeth, they'd be in some trouble. She told herself not to look at Stan's feet if he took off his socks. But there was something calculating in the way Sapphire perceived things and that made them more palatable. Through Sapphire's analytical eyes, Lynx saw this colorful, new world, taking it in much like any other piece of data to be processed.

*

By the time Stan and Sapphire made it to their reserved room, it was almost five p.m. Stan led Sapphire to the "red bed," as the girls called it, taking care to be extra sweet and soft-spoken. "You're beautiful, Sapphire. Prettiest girl in this club, not to mention the smartest. I wish I'd met you sooner." Suddenly, the mustard stain and fat seemed to melt away, although not so much the onion-dip breath.

"Thank you, Stan." Lynx looked into his blue eyes, trying to picture his soul rather than his appearance, wondering if a sex-crazed casino owner could ever be considered a good person.

Stan took off Sapphire's bra, staring at her breasts for a long moment. He began licking her nipples, and Sapphire thought, *so this is what he's into.*

"Can you lick mine, too?" Stan asked.

"Sure," said Sapphire.

Stan took off his shirt feverishly and sat on the edge of the bed, waiting. Sapphire got to her knees and licked one of his nipples, then the other.

"Harder,' Stan breathed—the smell of onions flooding Sapphire's senses. She sucked harder, as hard as she could, a part of her hoping he would suffer, but the harder she sucked, the more he seemed to enjoy it. His pants grew tighter as a large erection built up like a bouncy house inflating.

Stan stood up and stripped off his pants, taking Sapphire completely by surprise when she saw his choice of underwear. Of all the choices in the world, Stan, the king of sausage and casinos, was wearing a woman's pink velvet thong.

"Huh?" said Sapphire, almost laughing. She must have had a funny face because Stan felt the need to explain promptly.

"You'd be surprised how good an erection can feel in a pink velvet thong," said Stan. He smiled a boyish grin.

"Really? And here I thought you were making a side bet with one of your friends." Sapphire couldn't help smiling at the prospect of one of his friends losing that bet. This man was becoming funnier, and somehow more likable. There was a sad desperation to him, not so much a perverted one. This was a man who had submitted to his addictions and emasculated himself.

"No, it's something for me … and you. I know it's funny, but it doesn't mean what you might think it does," Stan added. "I have a healthy sexual appetite, Sapphire. I hope that's okay."

"There's no need to explain. That's why people come here, right? They're tired of hiding who they are, myself included," Sapphire tried not to hesitate in her response. She wanted to make her customers feel understood. From her personal experience, there was nothing worse than feeling unwanted and misunderstood. She imagined a man of Stan's size and aesthetic had experienced rejection, more than once in his lifetime.

Sapphire rubbed Stan's penis with her breasts, listening to his breath quicken.

"I need you to do me a favor," said Stan.

Sapphire looked up at Stan, her lifelike eyes hid the optical circuits inside. "Tell me."

"I need you to stomp on me," said Stan.

"Do what?" Sapphire read Stan's facial features, as well as his vital signs. He was warm, his heartbeat elevated and penis fully erect.

Stan lifted his head—face firm and resolute, yet full of desire.

"Come again?" said Sapphire.

"I want you to stomp on me as hard as you can," Stan repeated.

Sapphire counted out four seconds before she responded. "L-like how."

"Stand on me. Then, stomp on me … please." Stan choked up, a darting desperation in his eyes. He looked down at his crotch, nodding that she could stomp on his cock.

"With shoes or without shoes?" Sapphire stared at Stan. Back at home, Lynx looked down at her palms, aware of the home button that could take her out of this situation. She could not believe they were having this conversation. If only Sapphire could do this by herself in automatic mode. This was indisputably the most incomprehensible request she had ever heard, and she'd read a lot of wild stories in Neo Grid City's most obscure magazine, *Digisex Trends*. She recently read that ballbusting or cock trampling was trending, but she thought that was a myth, much like a golem or a leprechaun. But here in front of her was a man who wanted to be hurt—apparently, getting a psychological fulfillment out of being physically overpowered and humiliated by a female.

Lynx let that roll around her brain for a minute as she considered Stan's request and started to somewhat enjoy the thought. Stan the man, who apparently liked getting his balls destroyed. Sapphire decided she would neither condemn nor criticize Stan for this request. As a matter of fact, she would be the best ball buster in the club.

"Let's start without," said Stan, half muttering.

"Alright, then. Lie down," Sapphire commanded. She pulled herself up from the ground, stood on top of the bed, and took her shoes off before slowly placing her feet in front of Stan's face where he could see them.

"Oh," he managed, his eyes wide as saucers.

She took one foot and put it up to Stan's cheek, pushing his fat flesh up and around, massaging it. He moaned, and Sapphire moved down, carefully balancing herself, first on Stan's thighs, then his balls. Sapphire felt the balls of flesh below her feet, moving around like two small water balloons.

"Mmm," Stan sighed, his eyes rolling in the back of his head.

Sapphire intuitively understood that if Stan wanted to get the full effect of this cock trampling, she would have to jump, pushing her full weight down on him. She jumped up as high as she could and landed hard, smashing her heels into Stan's balls. She was uneasy at first and tried to avoid the phallus while letting the balls take the full front of her blow.

"Ahh," Stan moaned. This was a green light as far as Sapphire was concerned.

She jumped again, squishing down hard on his balls upon landing.

Stan moaned again, this time louder, "Mmm."

Jump … mmm.

Jump … ahh.

Stomp, stomp, stomp. Ahh, mmm, ahh.

This continued faster and in rhythm. Sapphire found herself grinding her feet into Stan, feeling empowered and overjoyed. A disturbing revelation hit Lynx back at the apartment as she realized her pussy was dripping down to her knee … she was a sadist, true and blue. Sexual sadism—when a person is sexually aroused by inflicting physical suffering to another human being, was usually brought on by … what?

Lynx tried to determine what could cause a reaction like this? *What was it? Oh God, of course,* she thought. Sadism is catalyzed by traumatic events during childhood. She stepped back in a daze, not realizing she'd stepped off Stan, who was shaking in front of Sapphire.

He struggled to speak again, "Sapphire? You alright with this?"

Breathing heavily, Sapphire said, "I'm better than alright. I'm … I'm loving this"

"Good. Then, by God girl, you have yourself a bona fide sugar daddy." said Stan.

"Shall I continue?" she asked.

"Hell, yeah."

*

After all was said and done, Stan paid Sapphire $20,000 upfront, which was more money than most people ever made in a month, let alone an hour. Sapphire realized her perception of Stan was now fully warped by material benefit. The more she thought about it, the more she found it endearing that he'd chosen to reveal his good ole' boy persona to her before shedding it like an old snakeskin. They stood gawking and smiling at each other as they stood outside the bathroom.

"I'll wait for you here," said Stan, chipper than ever.

"There's no need. I'm just going to freshen up before heading back down," said Sapphire.

"No, no. I insist. There's a killer on the loose and you'll be better protected. You'd be surprised what this fat ole' boy can do. I wasn't raised to be no sheep."

Sapphire chuckled. "Alright, if you insist." *After all, he paid for it,* she thought.

While Sapphire went into the bathroom, Lynx obsessed over the amount of money she had made, thinking about all the happiness it could buy her. She could finally tackle her credit cards and start an emergency fund. A manic confidence emerged as she imagined a nice house with a three-car garage. She could help her mother, putting her into a better facility.

Lynx tossed around all the possibilities as Sapphire fixed her hair and makeup in the bathroom mirror. She caressed her lips with her finger, feeling a cocktail of pleasurable sensations soaking through her. She was the adult in charge now—a pole dancer and proud of it. In that moment, Lynx owned her confidence and demanded the attention that was rightfully hers. She smiled at herself in the mirror one last time as she left the bathroom to find Stan, who was waiting patiently with his shirttail still untucked.

"Stan," said Sapphire. "I'm going to have to dress you better than this." She reached around Stan and tucked in his shirt, yanking his thong up his ass as she did so.

"Hey, now! Watch the thong," said Stan, clenching his butt cheeks and smiling.

Sapphire laughed. "Just testing the waters."

"To be continued next week? Say Monday? That can be our day," said Stan.

"Better have your safe word ready," said Sapphire. She winked, as she focused on the next $20,000.

"Shall I escort you to the main floor?" Stan popped in another lump of chewing tobacco and extended his arm toward Sapphire.

Determined to make Stan her "whale" customer, Sapphire took his arm, placing her arm inside his warm fat folds. She felt safe as Stan escorted her down the stairs and back to the action of the club. As they made their way to the main dance floor, Sapphire saw one of the girls arguing with a customer.

"Oh no. What do we have here," said Sapphire

"No idea. But you better walk behind me, Sapphire."

As Sapphire stood behind Stan, she felt confident that his fat alone would catch the brunt of any punch or kick. She felt the warmth of his big body and squeezed him from behind to let him know shw was ready.

The unruly customer was in the stripper's face, waving his hands around as if he was a conductor. As things escalated, they both stood up from their red velvet loveseat, standing face to face. He was short and stocky, almost the same height as the stripper with wavy black hair.

"I'm not a damn Tetherbot. I'm a real girl," said the stripper, pushing her tits up and together.

"Yeah right, Valentina. If that really is your name," said the stiff-necked, recalcitrant customer. "I'm not buying it. You seem off, and I'm not paying you or this trashy club."

"Ovidio, you've been to the Cyberbar before. You've seen me around … asked the other girls about me," Valentina replied, clutching her red faux-leather purse. "And now, you're being a cheapskate because you don't want to pay. You want something for nothing. I should have known better when the other girls said you don't buy dances." Valentina's purse seemed to melt into her body, matching her red dress and lipstick. Her long, black hair covered her average breasts. If she was fake, Sapphire would be surprised. She didn't think Tetherbot sold tits that small.

"Yeah, because I don't have to pay for pussy, especially not artificial pussy. If I wanted that, I'd go outside and hump my rubber tires."

"That's disgusting," said Valentina.

"More disgusting than that cum dumpster of a pussy? I think *not*," said Ovidio, chugging the rest of his beer.

"Go ahead. Drink some more, you cheap, short slush," said Valentina. "I couldn't even feel your small dick when I was on top of you. That's why you're really angry."

"I'll tip you if you're real. After you bleed, bitch!" With that, Ovidio took his empty glass beer bottle, placed it in his hand like a club and smashed it on top of Valentina's head. Red blood drained down her head, spilling into her eyes. She put her hand to her head, shaking and in shock.

Before anyone else could react, Stan rushed Ovidio with incredible speed, his big arms hulking. Stan reached back, and then released one huge overhand punch, connecting square in Ovidio's face. Ovidio flew back and over the loveseat before landing hard on the floor.

He rose to his feet, angrier than before, red-faced and breathing hard. Ovidio charged Stan, throwing punches into his fat body, which absorbed the hits like a king-size waterbed. Ovidio went in for the takedown but struggled as he tried to lift Stan. Stan countered with an elbow to his head, sending Ovidio to his knees.

Enraged, Ovidio grabbed another beer bottle as he pushed himself up, but Stan gave him a one-two punch in rapid succession, knocking Ovidio out cold. By this time, security was on the scene, and they started dragging Ovidio out of the bar.

The crowd clapped, amazed at Stan's prowess. The other patrons came to check on Valentina, who was sitting down, dabbing a napkin on her head.

"Are you alright?" said Stan.

"I'll be alright. Luckily, Ovidio is a weak ass," said Valentina, chuckling weakly.

Stan handed Valentina an undisclosed wad of cash. "Here, this should cover the medical expenses. Go home and rest. Come back whenever you feel better."

"Aww, that's so sweet. Thank you," said Valentina. She looked up at Sapphire who was now at Stan's side. "You're so lucky."

"Yes, I am lucky," said Sapphire. She looked at Stan with awe, slowly taking in a deep breath and releasing it. It wasn't because Sapphire needed air. It was because Lynx did. She was overwhelmed with the prospect of this man fulfilling her daddy complex.

Lynx put Sapphire on a quick pause, fumbling around her apartment for another MDMAX. She took half of a jagged pill and swallowed it, trembling. She hadn't expected anyone to stand up for a money-grubbing stripper.

Lynx unpaused Sapphire, and was back at it, stuck with an expanding feeling in her chest. She needed the MDMAX to kick in so she could disconnect with the world and numb the pain of swelling emotions.

"Sapphire?" said Stan.

"Yes?" Sapphire looked at Stan, unblinking.

"You good?"

"Yes, all good. I just needed a moment to process things."

"Do I need to give you a ride home?" said Stan.

"No, that's alright. Thank you so much, though. Maybe next time. Just take care of that punching hand, would you?" Sapphire said. She smiled at Stan admiringly.

"Yes ma'am, I will," he said. He quickly bent over, kissing Sapphire's cheek. "And I will talk to Hazza about beefing up security. We can't have another incident like this one."

He left, and Sapphire watched Stan walk away, noticing his wide-stepped gait. She smiled, feeling silly for liking this chunky, boyish man. Maybe she was in the wrong for not being attracted to Stan's physical appearance, but she was at least attracted to his personality, his money, and his morals, which was good enough for her.

Out of the corner of her eye, Sapphire detected movement. The crowd made way as Hazza appeared out of nowhere, rushing over to check on Valentina with concern washing over his face. "Hey, are you okay?" Hazza kneeled in his slim-fit sharkskin suit, looking directly into Valentina's eyes. "I'll be alright," said Valentina, trying to get up.

"No, no. Don't stand up too quickly. I'll get my men to help you," said Hazza, indicating with his finger for someone to help him. Braylen and Carney swarmed around Valentina, swiftly and gently lifting her up to assist. Hazza stood up, turning around to make fierce eye contact with Sapphire. She looked at him wide-eyed and curious, as if understanding some desperate need inside of Hazza.

"Sapphire," said Hazza, tipping his head. "Do you mind if we chat for a bit?"

"Me?" said Sapphire, pointing at herself.

"Yes, please. If you have a moment, that is." Hazza reached out his hand, gesturing for Sapphire to follow him. She grabbed Hazza's soft hand and followed him to a private office space behind a black door against the eastern wall. She had no idea this space was here, tucked off to the side of the girl's dressing rooms. Hazza pulled out a chair for Sapphire and waited for her to sit down. He walked around his desk and sat down in a red leather chair across from Sapphire.

"What's this about?" said Sapphire. She looked around the walls, expecting to find a certificate, or anything hanging on the walls—instead, it was bare, withholding any information about its mysterious owner or purpose. Sapphire thought this was strange; the bareness of it all reminded her of death. No pictures on the walls was surely a sign of depression, loneliness, or isolation. Was Hazza hiding something?

"I wanted to apologize to you," said Hazza, staring at Sapphire.

"Okay," said Sapphire. "For what?" She smoothed the left side of her hair, suddenly self-conscious of her appearance.

Hazza sighed, running his fingers through his dark hair. "I shouldn't have hired you."

"Huh? Why not?" said Sapphire. She scanned Hazza's desk, taking note of a laptop, two self-help books, and a USB charging port. The room was quite small for an office, not one suitable for a man such as Hazza, whose presence soaked up the entire room.

"I get the feeling this is personal. The killer is targeting me and my girls." Hazza shut his laptop, letting out a sigh.

"Hazza, this is not your fault. The killer is targeting the whole Cyber Brothel District."

"No?" Hazza stood up, staring off into the bare wall. "Then explain the fights, the killer, and the stalking."

The last word got Sapphire's attention. "What stalking?"

"I was followed home the other night, Sapphire. To my home!"

"How do you know?" said Sapphire.

"I was in a relationship, to be honest with you. With one of my girls. He's been on me since then … watching me," said Hazza.

"What? Hazza, why …"

"I know, not exactly kosher. I don't know if the killer was out to hurt me, hurt her, or wanted to hurt me by hurting her, but she's long gone, you see … killed by *him*," said Hazza.

"No," said Sapphire, shaking her head.

"I wish I was lying, but I don't think he'll stop there. I believe the killer will find anyone who has any connection to me. For this reason, I've kept my distance from you. But Sapphire, I must tell you, I'm wild about you, I really am. I know it's wrong, especially after what happened, but I'd like to get to know the real Lynx."

"Well, I work here … so that's something to think about," said Sapphire. She felt a hot blush overcome her whole body. Hazza was devastatingly handsome, and most likely rich, but she couldn't mix business with pleasure—could she?

"It's something taboo. But before you …" Hazza shook his head. "You've given me a reason to hope, Sapphire. You see, so much has happened … I've worked so hard to get where I'm at, but something is missing in my life. I need to see you, I need to be near you. I am mesmerized by you."

"Hazza," said Sapphire, looking at her hands. "You've given me a lot to think about. But I need to process this. You know how different I am. I have … baggage."

Hazza grabbed his chair and brought it over to Sapphire, setting it down, right next to her. He sat down, cradling both of her hands in his. "I will carry your baggage, and then some." The burning look in Hazza's eye was enough to charm the pants off of her, but she knew this was all wrong.

"Can I think about it?" said Sapphire.

"Yes, just think. If I could help catch the serial killer, then maybe things could be different."

Sapphire's heart began beating fast and furiously in her chest, making it hard to think straight. "Hazza, you can't take that responsibility for yourself. Your girls need you. This place needs you," said Sapphire. She felt the truth in that statement, but more than that, she wanted to deflect the attention away from herself. She was relieved when Hazza pulled his hands back, settling back in his chair. As he retracted, her heartbeat began to slow down.

"Shall I give you a ride home tonight?" said Hazza. Sapphire caught the hopeful lust in his expression.

"Hazza, I need time to think," said Sapphire. She smiled it off, consciously pushing away the temptation.

Hazza smiled. "That's what I like about you, Sapphire. You're smart. You think about things before you leap. You won't throw yourself at me like the other girls."

"And if I did?" asked Sapphire.

Hazza smirked, "Well, it would've been fun for a day or two, tops. Then, I'm sure someone would have gotten bored."

Sapphire chuckled quietly. "Yes, the grass would have been greener on the other side."

"I think the grass is just fine where I sit." Hazza looked up and down Sapphire's body, filling the air with sexual tension.

"I could say the same for you, Hazza," said Sapphire. "But for now, I've got to go."

"I could watch you go forever," said Hazza. "As long as you come back."

Chapter 5
Braylen

Ever since the second murder, Braylen knew a madman was on the loose. A sadistic killer was targeting sex workers—a typical MO for a serial killer. But what made this killer different was that he specifically targeted Tetherbots and their users. He tortured them before killing the bot and frying the user's brain. Braylen obsessively watched the viral video feeds of the victims, paying close attention to the masked man and his modified voice. There were no real leads, no fingerprints, and no trace substances left behind. It was common knowledge that Neo Grid City's police officers often generalized prejudices about Tetherbot strippers and were unclear whether they should help Tetherbots the same way they would help people. Because of this, there was little evidence to support any type of ongoing investigation. Braylen would have to gain access to the crime scene if he hoped to make any progress finding the killer.

Braylen took on the case because he needed the money, and the cyber brothel owners were willing to pay. "Catching the crazies," as he liked to put it, was what he was born to do. He'd always dreamed of being a detective—a regular Columbo or Sherlock Holmes. But that dream took the backburner when his fiance was murdered and he became the prime suspect. Even after clearing his name, he was blacklisted … so he did the next best thing: running his own P.I. business. With his tracking skills, he was able to find two missing teens, bring down a car theft ring, and ultimately catch his fiance's murderer … her own sister. But serial killers were the ultimate catch, and stopping one could propel his business to new heights.

"Hey, Harris! We need to talk," Braylen yelled out as he saw the detective walking down the street toward the parking lot outside the police station. Catching up and breathing heavily, he said, "I need to ask you a few questions about the murders."

"Oh God. You? You gotta' be kidding me … the fucking rent-a-cop."

Detective Harris was a fifty-something grizzled veteran of the Neo Grid City Police Force, sporting gray hair and a carefully trimmed peppered beard and mustache. "Look," he said, continuing his walk toward his car. "You have full access just like the rest of us, which in fact I hate, but we can't control the web. I'm not divulging any information to some out-of-shape alcoholic wannabe private dick." Detective Harris blew a nasty-smelling waft of cigarette smoke Braylen's way.

"If we combine our resources, we have a better chance of catching this nut before he strikes again," Braylen replied. "Why shut me out of the investigation when you're obviously in over your head?"

"Fuck you, you opportunist. Just get the hell out of here!" Harris said, poking Braylen in the chest with his index finger. "We don't want or need your help. Go back to your dime bag, flea market of an office, and stay there." He opened his car door, got inside his unmarked police car, and lifted off toward the skyway, leaving Braylen holding his hat so it wouldn't be blown off by the spinning propeller blades.

"Goddamn, no good cop! I'm going to catch this killer, and I'll be the hero in this city!" Braylen shouted, to no avail, as the car was already out of hearing range.

He walked back to his car, an older model Skyflyer. It looked dingy but was his favorite color, green, and still reliable. He fired up the engine and flew off, heading for the Cyberbar. He wanted to check "Baby" Blue's room again and get a closer look at some of the patrons there tonight. Braylen was sure the killer was a repeat customer because he needed to stalk his victims to identify who the Tetherbots were, which would take time to figure out because they were so damn life-like.

"Hey, any more parking spots there, Eddie?" Braylen yelled out of his window at the parking attendant as he flew up next to the window. The attendant was sitting in a booth about twenty feet off the ground connected to the high-rise parking structure.

"Yeah, I've got a spot saved just for you. Third level, row four. The normal fee." The attendant pressed a button and opened a gate to let Braylen through. Braylen gave him some creds and sped on inside.

After parking in his spot, Braylen made his way to the Cyberbar, which was a short walk down the city block. The street sidewalks were jam-packed with Tetherbots and young adults, either headed to work or running miscellaneous errands. Bikers weaved past Braylen in intersecting bike lanes as airborne cars and freighters flew overhead in procession.

It was a chilly night and a curtain of mist clung to Braylen as he walked toward the bar. The Cyberbar was glowing; the tiny rain particles bouncing from its signature neon lights were accenting the atmosphere like a blurry Monet painting. The holographic nude dancers were alluring, but they were faceless, reminding Braylen of the working girls who were exchanging their lives for a dollar inside. He had to admit, he knew the feeling of being broke and selling yourself all too well.

To get things done around here you had to grease the wheels. Handing a little cash to the right people led to quicker access. Braylen handed the bouncer in front of the Cyberbar a wadded-up $50 bill. "Anything new happening tonight? Hear any rumors there, Carney?"

"Yeah, I heard a few things," Carney said. "Hazza was here about an hour ago. He was pissed off on the phone yelling something about business profits being down."

"This place? Seems like easy money. I haven't noticed a dip yet."

"Not yet, but the girls are talking—some are saying they'll get a *real* job, whatever that means. Nowadays, nothing's really real, you know what I mean? Can't find a girlfriend before stumbling upon another Tetherbot. But yeah, Hazza seems more pissed than usual. More money, more hoes they usually say. But now it's all gone haywire, you see."

"What's Hazza expecting? With a killer in the city targeting the clubs, he's going to lose some."

"Yeah, everyone's on edge. We've got cops in here, surveilling the place and harassing the customers. Detectives are looking at boyfriends, grasping at straws trying to solve these murders. The killer has everyone on standby, it seems. We're on his time." Carney opened the door for Braylen to go inside.

"That's why I'm here. I'm on the case, and nothing gets by me …"

"Okay, Braylen. I feel a whole lot safer now," Carney said, smiling and laying the sarcasm real thick.

"You should. I'm the genuine article," Braylon called back as he entered the bar. The loud music and voices greeted him as he looked at the bartender and then briefly scanned the room. At first glance, everything appeared like a normal Friday night … girls stripping on the main stage, dancers on the floors, guys spending cash. The only thing different was the extra security, collecting data and capturing IDs upon entry, but not conducting any real police work from what Braylen could tell.

"Get me bourbon on the rocks. None of the cheap shit, Erin," Braylen called to one of the bartenders. He spun his wedding ring on his finger. He never took it off, even though Jenny had died five years ago.

"Fine, Braylen. But your tab is getting a little high," she replied. "I'm going to need some sort of payment soon."

"Here's a little something." Braylen slipped Erin a $100 bill, then grabbed her hand when she went to grab it. "Put it towards my tab, and then take a piece for yourself. But I need a favor. I need access to Blue's room."

"It's still sealed by the cops," said Erin, brushing her short, blonde bangs from her face. "They're not letting anyone in until they finish clearing it of evidence."

"That's why I need to get in there," he pleaded. "Those bozos will only fuck it up, and then Blue's killer will never be found. Do it for Blue." He removed his hand.

Erin stuffed the cash in her black bra, hidden under a sexy, black mini dress. She looked hesitant before reaching under the bar and presenting a small red keycard to Braylen.

He snatched the card and slipped it inside the left breast pocket in his jacket. He swung his bar stool slightly to the right to get a view of the main stage, sipping his drink. "Notice anyone strange tonight, Erin? Anything new catch your eye?" he asked without looking away from the stage.

"Nothing strange apart from the usual weirdos who came in," Erin said, grinning.

"Let me know if you notice something off. We have to stay vigilant. I'm heading in there after I finish this drink."

Braylen took a large swallow of bourbon. Out of the corner of his eye, he noticed a gentleman sitting alone at a corner table. The man was leering near the stage with his head downcast. He had a very gaunt, pale face with sunken eyes and was wearing a long black jacket over a gray shirt and black pants. There was little emotion on his face, which seemed suspicious to Braylen. It was a stripper joint with beautiful girls and music—who wouldn't be gawking? The man should be having a great time, but the guy looked like he was at a funeral.

"You notice that guy at that corner table? What's his story," Braylen asked after finishing the last gulp.

"That guy?" said Erin, tilting her head slightly in that direction.

"Yeah, him … I'm going to get a little closer, see if I can get a read on him," Braylen said as he stood from the stool.

"I've seen him here a few times," Erin said with a shrug. "Looks dark and mysterious but seems harmless. He orders drinks and tips well."

Braylen walked away from the bar and slowly strolled toward the main stage, keeping the strange man in his peripheral vision as he stopped and stood near the opposite side of the stage. The pale man barely seemed to move. Finally, he took a long sip from the drink sitting on his table.

"Work it, you sexy thang!" Braylen shouted out at Candis, who was dancing on the main stage. Braylen swayed and pumped to the beat of the music, masquerading as though he were one of the patrons. After the song ended, Braylen strolled away from the dance floor casually, never letting his eyes leave the pale man, who was looking distant and downcast as if in some far away land. The pale man looked out of place, but Braylen decided to head to Blue's VIP room, the scene of the crime instead.

"Excuse me. I have to take a piss," said Braylen to the bouncer, Gerald. Gerald crossed his arms, standing in front of the hallway leading to the VIP sections.

"Make it quick, okay?"

"Hey, Gerald. You know me, I'm taking a piss and then coming back to watch all the eye candy," said Braylen smiling, as he slipped a $20 bill into the crease of Gerald's folded arms.

"Just hurry up, Braylen. You're such a pain in the ass."

Braylen walked sideways past Gerald's hulking shoulders and made his way down the purple-walled hallway toward the bathroom and the room where Blue had taken her last breath. He stopped at the end of the hallway and turned left toward the VIP rooms instead of right to the bathrooms. Blue's room had been the second door from last, still plastered with bright yellow crime scene tape.

Braylen pulled out a small pocket knife. He cut through the tape and peeled it back to access the door lock, looking both ways down the hallway before entering. It was empty … not a soul in sight. He swiped the red keycard Erin had given him, opened the door, and entered carefully, closing the door quickly enough to stir up the stale air inside. Blue's room still had an electrical burn smell to it and the red velvet bed in the center was covered in silver robotic fluids, staining the red sheets. Before stepping forward, Braylen scanned the corners of the room, checking for security cameras. The cameras were active, moving slowly and filming the room. But Blue's video streaming equipment had been removed, along with all her clothing and possessions.

Braylen bent to one knee and started checking the shaggy carpet, looking around for any clues left behind. Then, he stood back up, combing the bed and the red couches encircling the bed. "Voila," he said, spotting some abnormal black fibers and a few blonde hair strands sticking to the velvety, red bed frame. He reached inside his blazer jacket and used his tweezers to place a few of the fibers into a small evidence bag.

Just then, the air conditioning kicked on, pushing out a dust-filled bloom of cold air in his face. Braylen coughed. He felt odd standing in the room, as if someone was watching him. He scoured around the room some more and, finding nothing, decided to leave before he was caught. He walked over to the door and began turning the handle.

Slam! Thwack!

The door flew right into Braylen's head, knocking him backward and onto his back. The door had been kicked in just as the bolt was released from the strike plate. Braylen was dizzied, but his adrenaline kicked in as he quickly scrambled to his feet, trying to focus on what was happening. He saw a fuzzy figure wearing black standing right in front of him. Braylen swung a right jab where he thought a face was and missed, swinging at air. He was then met with a stinging sensation to his right eye as a blow from what felt like a brick, connected flush with his upper cheekbone.

"Ahh, you fuck! Cheap shot," Braylen shouted out. His vision was completely gone on his right side and still blurry on the left. He struggled to locate the attacker, swinging fists in anger and frustration.

"You shouldn't have come here," the gravely distorted voice bellowed as the lights dimmed. Braylen was trying to take a defensive approach now, putting both arms up in a classic southpaw stance.

"Who are you? Did you kill Blue?" Braylen called out.

Braylen's left eye was beginning to focus. Out of the corner of the room, the devil-masked man dashed toward Braylen and delivered a one-hop sidekick to Braylen's ribs, knocking him to the plush floor. He lay in a fetal position wheezing, trying to catch his breath. Another kick came flying in, hitting Braylen in the arms, which he'd raised defensively. Three more kicks followed in swift succession, all striking his abdomen.

Braylen felt like he was going to puke, but after the third kick, he instinctively reached into his pocket for his small handgun. He quickly flipped the safety off and waited for another kick to come at him, but the kick never came.

With difficulty and breathtaking pain, Braylen got to his feet, standing slightly bent over, holding his ribs with one hand and his gun in the other. Suddenly, out of the shadows, a long needle darted towards him. He turned quickly as the needle pierced his skin and sliced a long red line across the side of his neck.

Braylen dropped his gun and jumped back as the needle twisted back into the dark. "Ahh, shit. My fucking neck. You damn coward!" Blood trickled down Braylen's fingers as he held his neck wound. It stung like a burn from a searing hot stove. He looked down, trying to find the gun, but his blurred vision made it hard to see in the low light.

Out of the dark, the devil mask appeared again, the connecting body was tall and thin, but Braylen already knew he was deceptively strong. This was it. He knew it was put up or shut up. Kill or be killed. Braylen pulled out his pocketknife and flipped it open.

"There you are. Now I can get a good look at a looney psychopath. A cowardice wannabe big shot," Braylen provoked the killer, trying to get a reaction.

"I don't think you're in any position to bluff." the devil-masked man said. "I know you're scared. You don't want to die. Not like this." He pulled out a sixteen-inch military knife from his long black coat, dwarfing Braylen's pocket knife as if it was a thumbtack.

"I'm not scared of anything, especially not a madman like you," Braylen said.

Suddenly, a knock at the door interrupted their discourse; Braylen answered it by yelling, "The killer is here! He's in here!"

The door knocks turned into bangs as someone began kicking the door, trying to smash it in. The devil-masked man turned to the door, leaving Braylen standing there with his knife. Gerald, the bouncer, was about to deliver another kick when the killer opened the door.

"Watch out!" Braylen yelled out, but it was too late. The killer plunged his knife directly into Gerald's chest, dropping him to the ground—then pulled the knife back out.

"NO!" With his back still turned, Braylen rushed at the killer and tackled him from behind, knocking them both down. They landed on Gerald's sprawled body, which was twitching and convulsing on the floor.

Having heard the scuffle, two working girls peeked out into the hallway from a VIP room, took one look at the body and screamed bloody murder. Braylen frantically grabbed at the killer's mask, trying to reveal his identity. He was met with a back-handed fist to the face, then a hard kick as the killer swiftly scrambled over Gerald's body. Blood gushed out as he pushed the corpse for leverage, leaving a blood trail across the killer's clothes as he got to his feet.

The killer looked around, then took off, running down the hall toward the emergency exit at the back of the building. Braylen struggled to crawl over the inanimate body, slippery and wet with sticky blood. Finally, after getting over Gerald and regaining his footing, he broke into a full sprint in pursuit of the killer.

"The killer … he's in the building. Get someone down here now!" One of the girls frantically shouted into her cell phone as the other girl rushed over to Gerald to see if there were any signs of life.

Braylen didn't look back; he kept running until he reached the double doors the killer had burst through only moments earlier. He pushed open the right-hand door and was met with a darkened alley. He couldn't make out much through his swollen right eye and he was adjusting to the darkness, but he could hear the killer's boots splashing through puddles down the roadway.

Braylen ran in the direction of the sounds to his right as he rubbed his eyes trying to clear up his view—his damaged eye returning a seething pain with every touch.

"Stop him! The killer's escaping," Braylen yelled out as he continued running, hoping a good Samaritan or patrolling security officer would help slow down the killer. He repeated this a few more times as he ran until he bumped into a crowd on the sidewalk, impeding his progress. "The man in the mask? Which way?" Braylen shouted. A couple of pedestrians pointed toward the road going westbound.

As his vision cleared up, Braylen was able to get a clear view of the killer, running and bumping into pedestrians and e-scooters as he shoved past them. The killer was a good city block ahead of Braylen, but he was having the same struggle navigating through the numerous pedestrians on the sidewalks. With impressive agility, the killer sidestepped the congested traffic onto the four-lane streets. Cars honked and whizzed past, swerving out of the way to avoid an accident.

"Get out of the fucking road!" yelled a driver who had almost clipped the killer.

Braylen pushed his legs harder and was gaining ground with each step as he swerved past the sidewalk pedestrians, cutting in and out of the street whenever the car traffic was low. Then suddenly, the devil-masked man turned and stared right at Braylen. His piercing eyes met Braylen's as he inched closer and closer. Braylen was within two arms' length of the killer in the middle of the intersection.

The killer tilted his head, turned, and ran full speed ahead with no intention of slowing down as he sprinted down the street. A red sports car barreled through the intersection, completely unaware of the pending collision.

BAM!

The driver crashed into the devil-masked man straight on. He flipped over the hood and slammed into the streamlined windshield, cracking the glass, and sending him sliding over the roof and onto the pavement. Braylen was there on the spot in seconds, breathless— huffing and puffing directly over the killer's body. Braylen grabbed the killer by the collar and lifted him by the neck. Sparks and smoke were emanating from his ears and mouth. The devil mask was broken in half, lying in a puddle of dirty curb water.

"It's a fucking Tetherbot! God damn, you dirty trickster," Braylen said, gathering himself, taking in choppy, labored breaths.

The driver of the sleek, red sports car got out of his vehicle to assess the damage to his front end to see what he hit. "What the fuck! That guy just ran into the street! He messed up my car, man!" The driver said, looking at the broken windshield and scrape marks on the hood and roof.

"Call the cops. DO IT NOW!" Braylen shouted at the driver. Even though he didn't trust the police, they had to clear the area and set up an official crime scene.

"I am, I am. Is he fucking dead?" the driver asked, turning his head and looking toward the back of the car. "Is that one of those Tetherbots? Oh, for fuck's sake. Those things are a damn menace."

The driver was still on the phone when a patrol cruiser dropped in from above, descending like a drone to land, flashing its emergency lights and blaring a siren. It hovered about ten feet in the air, disrupting the air with swirling wind from the propellers. The sirens stopped as a police officer opened the top hatch, revealing himself in his seat. "We got a call about an accident. Do you need paramedics," the officer said over his loudspeakers.

"I need you to contact Detective Harris. Tell him it's about his case and to get the fuck down here," Braylen hollered above the noise.

"Yeah? And who are you?"

"I'm Braylen Dempsey, P.I."

A crowd of rubberneckers shamelessly gathered along the sidewalk, getting louder and more restless as they ogled the scene.

"Okay. Everybody back up and disperse. Nothing to see here," the cop instructed over the loudspeaker. "Back-up is on the way. Move along or be fined."

Braylen knelt beside the fallen Tetherbot, thoroughly searching its coat pockets and pants. Finding what he was looking for, he got up from a bent knee and covertly slipped the killer's needle weapon into his inside jacket pocket. It was black and compact, resembling a slightly thicker ballpoint pen.

"Hey! Braylen! Get away from the scene! Don't touch anything. This is a police matter," the cop ordered over his intercom. As Braylen turned to talk to the cop, a beeping noise emitted from the bot. It wasn't very loud, but it was intermittent and proceeded to quicken in pace.

"This thing is going to explode. Get back, now!" Braylen yelled, scrambling to put some distance between him and the Tetherbot. As he reached the crowd, he began pushing the people back away from the impending detonation.

"Get back! We have an explosive device," the cop relayed over the loudspeaker.

The crowd panicked and people ran everywhere, pushing and knocking fellow passers-by to the ground.

As suddenly as it had started, the beeping stopped. The Tetherbot burst into flames with sparks crackling in a violent, electrical spectacle.

"Shit." Braylen raced to the flames, trying to stomp them out and save whatever evidence was left.

Coming from the flow of flying traffic, an unmarked, black sedan zoomed in and hovered down, coming to a direct halt. A puff of smoke proceeded Detective Harris as he exited the vehicle. "Braylen, you again? What the fuck happened here?"

"The perp jumped me at the club, so I chased him down here, where he got hit by a car. Turns out the killer was using a Tetherbot to commit his crimes," Braylen said calmly. He didn't want to give too much detail, knowing full well that he had violated the crime scene.

"That's quite a story," Harris replied. "What are you leaving out? I happen to know you were at my crime scene. We already got a call about the dead bouncer. The witnesses are being interviewed as we speak. They all ID'd *you,* leaving Blue's room with the bot here."

"Well, damn … you got me. I was just covering all the bases. That's what I'm paid to do," Braylen said.

"About that. Who's paying you? You never divulged who your benefactor is."

"You'll know in due time. I'm an open book," said Braylen.

The detective stared suspiciously into Braylen's eyes before responding.

"What you did … put others in danger and led to the murder of a security guard," Harris continued. "I should haul your ass in for trespassing and tampering with evidence." Harris pulled out some lip balm, applying it thickly around his lips.

"Do it then, and my lawyer will have me out the next day," Braylen said in a smartass tone. "You should be thanking me for bringing your tired ass one step closer to solving this case."

"You disrespectful shit." Harris's face turned red as he rushed at Braylen, pushing him back with a stiff shove to the chest. Braylen planted his feet steady on the floor. Instead of backing down, he held two fists out, ready to go. Harris charged forward, swinging his fist and grazing Braylen's lower jaw. Braylen gathered himself and turned to offer retaliation, but was met by other cops, who had converged on the scene. Four officers separated the two and held them back until they cooled off.

Once things calmed down, Harris and his unit checked the crime scene and gathered what evidence was left from the Tetherbot, directing a forensics team to sweep the area for clues to its origins.

"You're coming to the precinct right now," Harris spat at Braylen. "I want to question you personally about what you know and what you saw. Get in the car. I'll take you there."

"Is this a request?"

"This is a damn order, or I'll haul your ass to jail for unlawful entry!"

"I'm not going anywhere with you."

"Boys! Grab this son of a bitch and throw him in my car."

Two burly cops walked toward Braylen, ready to follow the detective's order with the utmost aggression, if necessary. The cops, who were more like cinder blocks than a police force, grabbed Braylen's arms and forced them behind his back, dragging him to Detective Harris' cruiser.

"Fine, fine. I'll go. Take your mitts off me," Braylen said. Braylen got into the black sedan with the Detective and took off, heading to the police station.

Chapter 6

Too Close to Home

It was Saturday morning, and Lynx contemplated taking a day off to decompress and rest. However, the thought of having nothing to do other than veg out and play video games didn't sound appealing. She was far too deep into Sapphire's parallel life for relaxation. She thought she could take Sapphire somewhere other than the club— maybe down the streets of Neo Grid City to find new friends or new adventures. She could go for a walk in the park and feel the gravel road beneath her feet, spinning down pine-lined roads on the outskirts of the city, where the vegetation was being resurrected among the stale runoff of the city.

Lynx was wondering when Stan would text or call, when there was an unexpected knock on the door. She opened the curtain to the window overlooking the parking lot and looked outside, paranoid about who it could be. Was it Hazza? Could it be nosey-ass Braylen? She didn't see a recognizable car on the street, but that didn't mean anything. Instinctively, Lynx took Sapphire to the bedroom and tucked her under her bed covers. She ran back to the living room, feeling breathless.

"Who is it?" she shouted, trying to tidy up the living room.

"It's just me," said a familiar husky voice on the other side of the door.

"Robert?"

"Open up, girl. I've been worried about you."

Sapphire opened the door to a frazzled-looking Robert. His long sun-streaked, shaggy hair was wild and windblown—a comforting sight. After all the years of friendship, Lynx never understood why they'd never become more than just friends. They had both grown up in the sprawling Suburban District on the outskirts of the city. It was a modest housing development filled with two-story cookie-cutter homes. They had attended the same schools and lived just a few blocks apart. They had gone out a few times in high school, but it never got more serious than a kiss.

That's as far as she wanted to remember back. She didn't want to remember her own failings, or his on-and-off-again girlfriend—a low-life waitress living in some insignificant, Podunk town. His girlfriend worked a lot and made the commute to see him, but something was always off, he had said. As a result, Lynx looked the other way as Robert conducted his affairs. She didn't know who he was with presently and knew better than to ask. Staying out of his relationships was convenient if she was being honest. It gave her more time to withdraw into her cocoon and nestle up in her home like a little hermit crab burying its head in the sand.

"I told you to text me when shit goes down," said Robert, leaving the door open a foot wide. "Why didn't you? The brawl at the club went viral on social media."

Lynx closed the door behind him swiftly. "I know, I know. I wanted to. It was a lot to take in, that's all." She looked down at her feet.

"Are you alright?" Robert studied Lynx's face, apparently checking it for bruises.

"I'm fine, I'm fine," said Lynx, pulling her clothes tighter. She missed Sapphire in these situations. Sapphire could absorb the stares with ease.

"Are you sure? Mind if I sit down?" said Robert.

"Of course, help yourself." Lynx swallowed hard, staring at Robert. She wasn't used to visitors, not in person anyway. Robert only made a habit of stopping by on holidays or special occasions—most likely because he knew she didn't have a family to speak of.

"So? How's it going, Lynx?" Robert put his arms up on the couch and settled in.

"It's been lucrative," she said. She propped herself down in the middle of the floor, crossing her legs.

"Yeah?" Robert moved his hair out of his face. He smelled rugged, like the breeze outside. Lynx liked it and imagined smelling his neck. *Ugh, I'm so lonely,* she thought to herself. This visit was good for her, but she was tense. She reminded herself, *I'm an explorer, ready to see the real world soon.*

"How many years has it been, Lynx?"

"About ten years, I think." said Lynx, shifting her legs.

"You know what I mean," said Robert. "How long has it been since you've left this apartment?"

"Oh c'mon, Robert. I moved in, didn't I? I had to leave then." Lynx crossed her arms.

"You had movers. The car ride here doesn't count," said Robert. "This isn't healthy, Lynx. You can't Tetherbot your whole life away. Now that you have Sapphire, I worry you'll never see the light of day."

"I'm good. I'm getting ready to go out soon. Just prepping is all," said Lynx, stroking her hair.

"Alright. Get dressed and show me. Let's go." Robert stood up, getting ready to leave.

"You know I can leave if I want to," said Lynx. Her eyes darted around the room, then to the window.

"I know it. So, show me." Robert jingled his car keys in front of Lynx.

"Not today. Today's no good. It's hot outside."

"Like hell it's not. It's as perfect a time as any. C'mon. Let's see it then." Robert helped Lynx up, nudging her gently.

"Well, I … you ask for too much. I don't see why it's such a big deal. You know what I went through last night."

"Exactly. It's not a big deal. Which is why I need to see if you can take care of yourself, should the need arise, especially since you don't call or text."

Lynx babbled incoherent excuses, before finally trotting off to her room to change. While she was changing, she heard Robert moving around. He called out, "Lynx?"

"Yeah?"

"You've got some heavy artillery in here," he said. Lynx blushed, trying to think of what she had lying around. Then she remembered the large, pink dildonic on the side of the couch. The haptic suit was tossed in the corner too, along with the VR headset. *Oh my God.*

She emerged from the room wearing baggy, black cargo pants and an oversized gray, graphic T-shirt, which she had tucked in. She swallowed the ensemble with an even bigger black cardigan. Robert roamed to the fridge and opened it, only to find milk and water, but nothing indicating proper nutritional intake. He looked in the pantry and found it scarce, with only three items: cereal, almond milk, and old, oily peanut butter. Robert shook his head and closed the fridge. "Lose the jacket," he said as he turned around and examined her.

"What? I like covering up. My hands get cold, and I like to warm them up in my pockets."

"We are not doing this, Lynx." Robert touched her shoulders with both of his hands. "We are moving forward, never backward. We are breathing, not holding our breath. We are fearless, not thinking about the unknown dangers. They are always there. We are submitting to them willingly, which is a whole lot different than cowering. You get me? You do not need to be tethered to anything. You are perfect as an imperfect human."

Lynx bit her bottom lip and nodded, slipping out of her black cardigan, which fell to the floor.

"Okay, that's good. You're doing good. Just look into my eyes. I've got you. Here, hold my hand. You trust me?" Robert extended his hand, never breaking eye contact.

Lynx turned her eyes away, clutching her purse in her right hand. She consciously forced her limbs to relax as she set her left hand within Robert's warm right hand. There was comfort in that, at least.

"Alright, we're off. You have your key?" he asked.

Lynx nodded with a dry throat, breathing deeply.

"Okay, let's do this." Robert led the way down the apartment stairs, where they were met by the smells of deep-fried cooking and old cigarette smoke. Lynx could hear big dogs barking and the neighbors' yells echoing down the hallway with the breeze as they shuffled down the steps and to the ground floor. A door slammed and someone distracted by their phone rushed by, nearly knocking into them. Lynx gasped, trying to breathe again.

"It's okay, Lynx. These people are just like you, more than you know—running around trying to make ends meet in a busy world ruined by either social media or technology. The technology all around us binds us to this earth, now more than ever. Look at how it separates us." Robert pointed to the vehicles in the sky, then the street traffic, then to the Tetherbots and the people glued to their phones.

"Okay," said Lynx, shakily. She looked around Neo Grid City, taking it all in. The differences in income could be determined by the user's choice of vehicle, and whether it was airborne, or road bound. Hybrid aircrafts purred effortlessly overhead, gliding down to their designated runways, while motor engines puttered about the street, their heavy exhaust fumes adding to the polluted air. Lynx subconsciously observed people walking to and from work, finding it both soothing and disturbing.

The same dichotomy could be observed between humans and Tetherbots. Humans walked around lost and dejected, sun-blistered, and malnourished, limping or missing teeth, while the Tetherbots walked around effortlessly and beautifully in the daylight, strutting like gazelles, with unnaturally perfect hair—not one thing out of place.

Across the street, a working Tetherbot was being beaten by an angry mob, and cops were rushing to the scene. Lynx understood why Tetherbots chose to fly in *Blueships*, opting to stay off the hate-ridden, crime-filled streets. More than that, Lynx saw the violence the Tetherbots indirectly caused.

She and Robert stood at the crosswalk, waiting for the green light to turn. "I thought you liked Tetherbots," she said.

A car honked at them, and the driver pointed impatiently for them to cross the street. Robert pulled Lynx's hand, and she shuffled her feet to keep up. His stride was surprisingly long and fast, and his grip was stronger than expected. Lynx observed his body as he walked ahead, stacked with lean muscles. *He's been working out.*

"I play the game like everyone else," Robert shouted over the street commotion. "But playing the game doesn't make me relevant. I'm nothing when I'm in my Tetherbot, only a shadow of a man. I carry out various tasks with ease … play the games I need to play, but I operate under the rules that Tetherbot creates. And as much as I love games, the power to choose is slowly being drained from us. This is no longer fun and games, Lynx."

Robert reached the end of the crosswalk and made a left, passing two street taco trucks.

Lynx registered the smell and her mouth began to water. "I'm hungry," she said.

"I bet. I saw your kitchen. You should have asked me for help." Robert stopped walking. He looked at Lynx while people walked past in both directions.

"Oh stop. I'm good. I was planning on ordering groceries soon. Where are we going, anyway?" Lynx looked around anxiously. *Why won't he get on with it?*

"Yeah, you keep saying that, but I'm not buying it. Ask me for help, Lynx. Just ask," said Robert. His eyes bore into Lynx's, penetrating her in a way that made her feel like he knew her inner thoughts and feelings.

"Help me with what?" said Lynx, squirming.

"Mm mph, nope. Don't do that." Robert's face twisted as he shook his head.

"Do what?"

"That thing where you pretend nothing's wrong. Like you can't get close to anyone."

"But I am who I am, broken and all." A pedestrian pushed past Lynx, and she clinched her hand to her heart.

"Lynx, I know you don't act like this with your customers. You'd never sell a dance if you did. You can be vulnerable with me. You know that." Robert stopped and looked around with a pained expression. "You know what? Just forget it. C'mon, let's go. Let's get to the heart of it."

Robert grabbed Lynx's hand and led her past a few resale tech shops packed to the brim with recycled VR equipment and Tetherbots. He seemed to be en route to the downtown district, where Tetherbot's headquarters towered over the supercluster of skyscrapers around it. As they approached the élan of the city, the shopping areas were bustling, stacked with rows of office buildings, warehouses, and tall balcony apartments outlining the paved streets. Within this urban jungle, street vendors shouted out their daily deals, showcasing food and trinkets. Tetherbot employees had long since ditched the corporate business suits for tight-fitting, black haptic uniforms. Here, Tetherbot's employees ate, slept, and worked—a concentrated area of shiny black suits, walking around like busy black ants working in mutual harmony.

"Where are we going, Robert?"

"I want to show you something," he said.

"But this is as far as I've ever traveled." Lynx focused on her steps, counting them to control her anxiety.

"It's worth it. Trust me." Robert took a left turn down an industrial alleyway that led to a lone brown door nestled in an old warehouse. "Here we are," he said, opening the door with his watch.

He led her down a poorly lit hallway, funneling into an abandoned commercial space with considerable square footage. There were at least fifty people in makeshift beds, starved with bedsores, being fed through tubes, and tended to by volunteers. A woman was talking loudly amid the overlapping voices and groans, looking oily and unbathed—her hair appeared to be dark brown with a bright blue streak in front. "This is where the future of robotics has taken humanity!" she yelled. "To a place where mods aren't available to help our loved ones. We are soaking in environmental uncertainties and poverty ... forced to become a basic component of Tetherbot's new generation robot. The robots of the future will learn autonomously, possessing qualities like self-maintenance to care for *themselves,* not *you. You* won't get a new model. *You* will be left like trash. The proof is right here, all around you! This is science, not speculation."

"What the hell is this, Robert?" said Lynx.

"Our human species requires physical touch for survival. We cannot become puppets to the corporate ventriloquist," the blue-haired woman continued. She looked to be in her mid-forties, a classic beauty ruined and beaten down by life's tribulations. Each wrinkle added to her dialogue, expressed through the crevices and furrows of her face.

"This is what becomes of Tetherbot users, Lynx. Or should I say Sapphire," said Robert. Lynx stared at his face in shock. An animated passion filled his eyes as he touched Lynx lightly. Feverish moans and coughs resonated through the expansive scope of the industrial space, and Lynx found herself totally overwhelmed.

"Robert, I'm scared," said Lynx. Looking around the vast space, she felt dizzy.

"You should be scared. You see this lady over here? Her name is Gemma." Robert walked over to an older lady on a bed; she was skinny and frail and barely breathing. "She's suffering from migraines, malnutrition, and cardiac arrest. She had to work twelve-hour shifts with her Tetherbot just to make rent after her husband died. These people can't *deal* with the real world once they are assimilated into their Tetherbots. They are *bound* together. Their bond to the Tetherbot is *so* strong that they are never able to integrate back into society. My colleague, Ginger, is trying to reprogram them. Listen, I wanted to tell you sooner, but I knew it wouldn't be easy. You had to see this for yourself. I had to show you, Lynx. You're the only constant in my life."

"Robert," said Lynx, looking down at her shaking hands. "What do you want me to do? I don't know what you want from me."

"I am a volunteer here, Lynx. I come here to help these people … the people whose lives have been stolen by the T-bots. I care about you, Lynx. I can't watch you turn into this. Join our cause. You can help us spread the word. We can *show* people what's happening. The public has the right to know, but Tetherbot pays off the media to keep the real stories off the streets."

The blue-haired woman came over and joined Lynx and Robert.

"Brought a new volunteer, Robert?" She wore a tight-fitting shirt, exposing her muscular frame.

"Hey, Ginger. Meet Lynx. I wanted to bring her over … show her what's happening to these people." Robert slicked his sun-streaked hair behind his ears.

"Nice to meet you, Lynx," said Ginger. "We sure hope you will join the cause. These people need help, but the funding for proper medical equipment has been an issue, so anything helps."

"I had no idea. These poor people," said Lynx. She couldn't feel her hands or the tip of her tongue—the tell-tale signs of her impending anxiety attack.

"Most people don't know about the long-term effects of Tetherbot use," said Ginger, petting Gemma's hair. "These bots can send you into a state of vegetation … a never-ending dream. Our aim is to reprogram the T-bot users and assimilate them back into society so they can function on their own again."

"It could happen to anybody, Lynx," said Robert. "They get into your head. Tetherbot has ways to get their consumers physically addicted to their headset and haptic suit. We don't know how the company does it, but we are trying to figure that out."

"This sounds crazy, Robert," said Lynx, covering her mouth.

"It's not crazy; the T-bots will be autonomous in the future. At what point do *we* end and *they* begin?" said Ginger. She put her hand on her side, where she was concealing a small handgun.

"I don't know if I can do this," said Lynx, breathing harder. She bent over, putting her hands on her knees.

"Lynx, breathe," said Robert, putting his hand on her back.

"I don't believe it," Lynx said. "This is crazy! People use Tetherbots all the time. We would've heard about it. Look, Robert, I know you mean well, but I'm using Sapphire. She's my ticket out of that crappy apartment and into a glamorous house in the hills, alone and away from everybody. And I can help my mom too."

"You need to listen to me. I'm trying to protect you," said Robert, in a soothing tone.

"Robert, I don't need you to protect me. I'm fine by myself. I promise I'll take more breaks and go outside as myself more often. But for now, I'm staying the course." With that, Lynx turned and quickly walked back the way they'd come.

"Hey, wait. I'll take you home," Robert called out.

"No. No need. I'm catching a *Blueship*. I already requested one when we opened the door."

"Wow. Nice friends, Robert," said Ginger, walking away to do her rounds.

Chapter 7

Make Money or Die Trying

It was midday on Sunday when Stan called Sapphire back to work, a whole day early. The message read, *Meet me in the VIP room. I'll be waiting for you at 2 pm. I can't wait to see you. XOXO, Fat Stan.* Back at home, Lynx chuckled at the Fat Stan reference and headed to the kitchen. She opened her orange unmarked pill bottle, eyeing the MDMAX pill in her palm before tossing it carelessly into her mouth.

"This should do nicely," she said, taking a drink of water. She tasted the bitter metallic taste of relief, which would allow her to live one more day without anxiety. One more day of beating the demons inside of her. One more day without asking for help, without going to rehab, or worse, becoming hospitalized like her mom. As the minutes ticked by, dopamine, serotonin, and norepinephrine became her symphony, stroking and playing her body like a grandmaster.

Lynx took a deep breath in, and a huge wash of relief filled her chest, her lungs, and finally her lady parts. Warm to the touch, she downed a whole glass of water. Then she drank another.

Sunday was fetish day at the club, so Lynx found her best S&M outfit for Sapphire, dressing her in an obnoxious purple strap-on dildo and matching outfit. She didn't think the dildo would cause her any problems, except perhaps on the awkward walk inside. Even so, she thought Stan would laugh and maybe enjoy it, since he was into pain. The worst-case scenario was that Stan would be offended and tell her to take it off. Either way was good with her, although she was in the mood to use it to punish someone other than herself today.

Welcoming this sexually perverted distraction, Lynx put on her haptic suit and her headset and finished getting ready through the eyes of Sapphire, despite Robert's warnings. *Robert exaggerates,* she thought. There is no way that all those Tetherbot users had been hurt at the hands of Tetherbot. Tetherbot would have no choice but to admit fault, recalling millions of robots and paying out hefty legal fees and damages. It would put them out of business without any chance of recovery. If it were true, she would lose her beloved Sapphire. *There is no way,* thought Lynx again.

*

Sapphire stepped out of the idling *Blueship* and slammed the door harder than she intended to—the effects of MDMAX running through her veins. It was 2 pm when Sapphire arrived at the Cyberbar, so she quickly made her way to the dressing room to finish getting ready. She took off her overcoat, revealing her shiny purple dildo. That's when she spotted Candis making her way over, wearing a sexy nun outfit.

"Wow, looking hot to trot," said Candis, flicking the dildo with her hand. "I might have to take you up on some of *that* later."

"Yup, all lubed up and ready to go. You're looking mighty fine yourself," Sapphire smiled, taking note of the nun headpiece, the collar, and the sexy cross stockings.

"Hot date tonight?" asked Candis.

"If you consider Stan hot," said Sapphire.

Candis gave a little snort. "Psh, as if. But it was nice what he did for Valentina the other night. Poor Valentina … she's all shook up."

"I can imagine. That was so scary. I'm glad Stan was there to help."

"Yeah, he made sure Valentina doesn't have to worry about anything other than flicking her TV remote for the next few months. I've seen the gifts he buys his girlfriends. Brand new cars? Trips? It's like, shit … get out of town … literally."

"I wouldn't know … at least, not yet. We only met one time," Sapphire said quickly.

"No problem. Just remember us little folks if he's strung out on one of those sharing moods. Remember … sharing is caring."

"Sounds good. You be careful out there," said Sapphire. She put her bag in her locker, grabbing her signature clutch purse, complete with lipstick, a small brush, feminine wipes, mace, and a mini laser knife. She had her watch, which served as a phone, so she didn't need anything else. Self-defense was the most important variable, given all the murders that took place.

"You too. Let me sync up with you and share my number. I'd love to help. We had fun last time, didn't we?" Candis winked, clinking her watch with Sapphires. *Bing*—the number was shared in bright pink colors.

"Yeah, we sure did." Sapphire flushed and cleared her throat, closing her locker. She didn't think Stan would even do threesomes, considering his ball busting fetish, but what did she know? There was still a lot to learn about him. Most of these freaks had something up their sleeve. After carefully studying Cyberbar's complete menu of services, she knew there were plenty of men who possessed a multitude of fetishes.

"Okay, then. I'm off. Say your prayers for me," said Candis, laughing at her pun. She made a praying gesture with her hands and smiled broadly, walking out of the dressing room and onto the dance floor.

Sapphire carefully avoided any of the other working girls, walking up the stairs slowly to the VIP area. She texted Stan on the way there, aching to meet and please her benefactor. She was in the mood to fuck him if he wanted, which was an unusual sensation, considering she never felt that way before owning Sapphire.

She analyzed the reasons for these newly acquired urges. Anticipating cash seemed to elicit a deep response—like a warm security blanket within her. Money was the ultimate power, affecting social status, happiness, security, love, and freedom—just to name just a few. In an economy where you could get anything and everything if you paid the right price, Sapphire was calculating a running total of all the things she could buy with this ultimate liquidity. One handy dandy feature Tetherbot users typically invested in, was top-dollar streaming services to publish sexual content on, ensuring steady royalties for the rest of their life. Maybe that's why she was thrilled to meet Fat Stan: He could buy everything she needed. *Stan, the sugar Daddy. Daddy,* Lynx thought. *Daddy.* She rehearsed a few clever stories in her head, desperate to please him, hardly noticing that she already opened the VIP door and stepped inside.

"Stan, I have a surprise for you today," said Sapphire in a sing-song voice. She whirled around, aiming her purple dildo to the sky only to see a slumped Stan, bending down in an unnatural way over his own tits and body fat. Blood was pooling beneath him. It occurred to her that she might be staring at a dead body while wearing a giant dildo—a grotesque juxtaposition. Sapphire stood there, registering the grizzly bloody scene, trying to pick up Stan's temperature and heartbeat. The Tetherbot could distinguish the difference between life and death and detect blood pressure with a simple touch. Sapphire had no need for these features before this moment—no need to detect life or death. The shock switched to alarm, and the thought of screaming finally crossed her mind. Sapphire was opening her mouth, awaiting the scream that hadn't quite come yet. She inhaled deeply, with her mouth agape.

"You scream … I shoot," said a tall, dark figure from the corner. "Besides, why do you care about this fat meat sack? Stan was the perfect sacrifice. He embodied everything, supporting cyber-prostitution." Out of the shadows, the devil-masked man revealed himself from his corner hiding spot.

As she shivered, the hairs on Sapphire's arm stood up, turning into goose bumps on Lynx's arms back at home as well. The devil-masked man was tall and dark—he was the fear that Lynx had lived with her entire life. He represented everything that made her afraid … everything that had kept her home. He moved farther into the light, exposing a long, dripping needle in one hand, and a gun in the other. He felt so close, so real. The idea of flight or flight occurred to Lynx, causing Sapphire to twitch in anticipation.

"I don't want to hurt you, Lynx. But you give me no choice." The light rested on the masked man's forehead, exposing the black shadows in the sockets of his eyes.

"How do you know that name?" asked Sapphire.

"I've been watching you. You're another Tetherbot, tricking unsuspecting people," said the killer. He lowered the gun and pointed the needle at Sapphire.

"Who are you? Why are you doing this to us?"

"I'm someone exposing the truth. Tetherbots are a scourge on society. I'm saving you by releasing its grip over your soul," said the killer. He was holding the needle weapon, bracing it against the end of his index finger accusatory, extending it towards Sapphire's neck like a long fingernail.

"Wait … *Robert?* Is that you?" Sapphire asked. "The voice … is distorted, but it sounds like you in there."

"I tried to show you. I tried to save you."

The needle twisted faster and faster, penetrating Sapphire's neck and paralyzing her instantly. She stood immobile like a mannequin in a boutique shop. Her mouth was open, her features frozen in a plastic coma.

Back at her apartment, Lynx managed to haul her headset off a second before the needle struck Sapphire, barely escaping the same fate as Blue. Leaving Sapphire to the killer was eating at Lynx, but she had to move on. She knew Robert was the killer—down to her core. He knew exactly where she lived and would be coming for her any minute now. Lynx removed the haptic suit and put her clothes on, rushing to find items she normally didn't use because she didn't leave home, like denim jeans.

She felt as if she was in automatic mode as she moved about her apartment, wondering, *what would Sapphire do?* This small bit of comfort was hardly a comfort at all, considering Sapphire had either been paralyzed or destroyed by Robert. This bothered her almost as much as finding out that her best friend was out to kill her. What has happened to Robert over the years? Lynx thought back to when she first started to notice a change in him. It was around the time he started dating that girl … Vannoy, was it? Lynx struggled to recall the name. *Damn the drugs. I can't remember where you strayed, Robert. My only friend. Why did it have to be you?*

She struggled with the old memories flashing through her mind, seemingly lost down the drain. Everyone had left her or hurt her, and now her only friend wanted to kill her. Given her family history, she knew she shouldn't be surprised about the betrayal. But to have a friend who knew her struggles and was trying to kill her anyway? Lynx forced herself to think of the murders, instead of her own selfish perspective. Robert needed to be stopped … and she would have to be the one to stop him. Where could she find the strength to beat her best friend without Sapphire? Her thoughts destabilized into prose form, diversifying, and breaking up into a fragmented oblivion.

Lynx took a whole MDMAX, muttering a poem to herself as she paced around her apartment.

I'm sitting here in my small, congested cell.
My body? I'm unaware it's here.
Yet I turn around in a deep fear.

Seeing your love,
Getting a glimpse.
Just observing,
Thinking it could have been.

Yet the clock is still ticking,
And the watch on my hand,
Says time is up,
No more quarter past ten.

But my soul is still here,
It rises and floats away.

Did it cross your path?
Did it call your name?
Did you try to catch it?
Did it do the same?

Or it could have flown by without a moment to spare.
And you never felt the love that should have been there.

I guess we'll never know,
I'm flying like a leaf,
Then all has been said but,
"Rest in peace."

After spinning in circles, Lynx knew she needed help. The pressure was too great. Her head felt like it was splitting at the surface. She couldn't do this alone … not anymore. To save herself and countless others, she would have to do things she was unwilling to do before. She packed a bag with her VR headset and haptic suit, along with her pills, a few changes of clothes, a toothbrush, her purse, keys, and some chargers.

Then she spoke into her watch and said, "Call Braylen."

Chapter 8
Killing Karen

Robert Chaise was an adjunct technology professor at Neo Grid City University, well versed in robotics and Tetherbot technology. He had worked there for two years but was recently fired for "insubordination." In his opinion, the real reason for his termination was his increasingly vocal perspective on Tetherbot utilization. Robert believed they should only be used for dangerous and repetitive jobs that people didn't need to do. This was one of the many reasons he loathed the company and its creations. Any statement against Tetherbot Corporation seemed to get buried in the sand, along with any other immoral infractions.

Robert worked quickly at his little corner tech table in his secret den, hacking the captured Sapphire through his VR headset. "Lynx, you should have listened to me. They all should have listened to me. Tetherbots are evil and will corrupt your soul. Now I must free you—like all the others." The intensity of his voice combined with the sing-song way he spoke, put Robert in another category, making him sound like someone in desperate need of a mental institution. Suddenly, as he stared into Sapphire's eyes, a whole new person was speaking. Robert was in a trance.

He glanced around his mundane home: his walls were decorated with awards and college degrees and his home office was quite tidy.

Nothing in his home screamed, "a serial killer lives here," in this quiet, suburban dwelling in the outskirts of Neo Grid City among stacks of cookie-cutter Edwardian terraced homes. The house was old, and it needed as much maintenance as a middle-aged woman in search of Botox injections during a midlife crisis. His mother had left the house to him—the only thing she ever gave him other than bruises and neglect.

At first, Robert had planned to leave the country to move away from the dirty cyber brothels and big tech companies that were taking over the lives of everyday citizens. But why run? He was a city-bred, highly educated technology guru, not some farmer. Instead, he had vowed to stay and force the necessary changes to the world. The day for a digital detox was here. Tetherbot's customers were referred to as "users," like drug addicts waiting for their next IV micro-drip. It was his purpose to free these hopeless users' souls and permanently rid society of the T-bot enemy. He was the only one who could do it.

No more fake online identities, no more romance scams, and no more heartbreak, Robert thought. He reflected on one girl in particular … Vannoy. She had been perfect—the only woman Robert had ever loved. He courted her for months, taking her out on the town to nice dinners, dancing parties, and parks. He'd been ready to settle down for once in his life. He'd gone as far as buying a ring—a fancy diamond one with emeralds, much like her eyes that could floor him right down onto one knee.

However, instead of the beautiful surprise engagement he had planned, a different kind of surprise unfolded and self-destructed in his face. Vannoy turned out to be a scam artist who'd bewitched him into falling in love with a Tetherbot. When he caught up with the "user," he had been shocked to discover it was an unattractive, elderly woman. He was heartbroken to learn that Vannoy was not Vannoy, his first love. She was Karen. And she was his first kill. Killing Karen was like any other magical first time: the first time driving a car, the first time going to prom, the first kiss, or losing your virginity. It was all that, plus more. The feeling of power that had surged through him was something unparalleled.

Karen had put her arms on Robert's shoulders, begging him for forgiveness, and more importantly, begging him for her life. The struggle had been so personal that he didn't think to use a needle … not for the first time. Instead, he'd reacted purely out of instinct, choking Karen until all the color in her face drained out completely. He watched her eyes turn from white to red, exploding within the spectrum of petechial hemorrhages. Love hemorrhages, as Robert liked to think of them. It was no different than a hickey, turning from a bluish purple, to green, yellow, and brown in the body's attempt to heal the broken, bloody capillaries right under the fragile neck. Robert had imagined Karen's vulnerable carotid artery, rushing her blood back from her head to her heart until finally, it had stopped beating. He alone had ended her blood flow—and he alone had played God.

He had to admit, he hadn't foreseen the sexual satisfaction he experienced at the time—his erection had been hard pressing against her body as she exhaled her very last breath. Everything had slowed during those moments before delivering death. Robert had become the master of time … the master of life. But he didn't want to free her soul, so he decided to keep Vannoy as a trophy, forever tying Karen to it. In his mind, Karen was trapped inside Vannoy—as long as Vannoy lived.

Robert quit tinkering with the headset and left Sapphire's body face down on his desk. He walked over to his bed, where two vacant Tetherbots were lying face down in the covers. "What do you say? It's almost July, Vannoy. Aren't you ready for the next kill? I know I sure could go for another angel face lying underneath my covers at night. Or do you think three is a crowd?"

Robert smiled, pulling the covers off Vannoy, exposing a bare Tetherbot, who had seen better than her shitty plastic days with Robert. Like an overused credit card, she was worn in intimate places, beaten, and neglected by anyone's standards. Next to her, lay Audry, a sultry, short-haired redhead, who had taken even more of the brunt of beatings than her robot roommate.

Vannoy and Audry had been modified with autonomous advanced A.I., which Robert had perfected over the last few years. Despite their worn appearance, they were more than old Tetherbots … they were his security force and his "wives."

Robert liked the comfort of sleeping next to someone, and as much as he hated these bots and everything they stood for, they served as a reminder of his mission when he woke up each morning. Sometimes he'd punch one of them and laugh; other times he'd have sex with one or the other—but usually, he woke up completely void and flatlined, unable to feel anything within a gray parallel universe that ignored all feelings. Any shred of humanity that he possessed had been stomped on and extinguished by Lynx, as if it were a small, smoldering ember. Lynx was the one person he thought would understand—the one person he could count on. But apparently, she wasn't on his side … not anymore.

While thinking about Lynx disturbed Robert greatly, thinking about Braylen infuriated him to the point of seeing red. He couldn't believe that a drunk, corrupt P.I. had taken down his main skin—the devil-masked T-bot. Robert's brain envisioned all of Braylen's possible deaths like a corny commercial replaying over and over—the one where you can't get the jingle out of your head. In fact, Robert would sing his little jingle, *"Death by stabbing, shotgun, needle, annnnd … strang-u-la-tion. "* It always made him giggle. Simple joys like this reminded him that he was only at the beginning of his long, promising, mission-oriented killing spree—and Braylen was clearly in the way of his mission.

Robert dressed in his haptic suit. Hearing the familiar zip amplified his adrenaline like that freakish friend trying to convince you to carry out naughty deeds. It was during that first zip when the rituals began. He had to admit, there was an arousing component attached to his rituals, since he imagined killing the girls again and again as he had sex with their Tetherbots. A man has his needs, but those needs were secondary to the bigger picture.

Robert thought about the simple dynamic of unity within Alcoholics Anonymous, which he tried adopting at one point to stop the killings after they first began. But instead of all that nonsense, Robert adopted his own principles to stand united for the greater good, only succumbing to his sexual fantasies *after* each kill was completed. By then, his sexual desire was so great, he felt like he might explode. To keep his principle, sedating his cravings was necessary, so he used the time in between victims to stalk—researching his next victim in the clubs. At the rate he was going, he could kill one girl a week, which was great progress.

Robert put on his VR headset and took control of Sapphire the same way he had taken control of the other Tetherbots. As Sapphire, Robert stood up and brushed her hair back. Still wearing her sexy cyber brothel outfit and knee-high boots, Sapphire walked over to Robert's family picture hanging on the wall and pressed a button under the frame. The wall slid open, revealing a cache of guns.

Chapter 9

The Precinct

Braylen was led inside the tan concrete Neo Grid City Police Department by Detective Harris with his gun on his hip. A long administrative desk sat in the lobby with a New American flag on one side and a blue and green city flag adorning the other. In the middle of the lobby was a city map, complete with aerial and ground transportation routes. The center of the city was where everything intersected and branched out, including the subway and all electric, hybrid and aerial vehicles alike. But it was also clear that the Neo Grid's city planners constructed people-first streets, prioritizing electrified bikes, scooters, and walkers in-transit for their frequent commutes to and from work. Braylen had seen a map of the city before, but with smarter energy sources and technology constantly transforming transportation, it was hard to keep track of all the latest updates in mobility.

Detective Harris walked ahead of Braylen, stopping to talk to a big-haired, big-hipped middle-aged lady, who was sitting behind a window in front of a touch screen computer. "Hey, Elsie. How's the husband?" said Detective Harris, itching his arm.

Braylen looked down, noting two sharp scars lining Detective Harris' wrist, consistent with punching a window. *His damn hand must have gone clear through a glass window,* Braylen thought. *Big surprise ... Detective Harris has a bad temper.*

"As good as any old grump could be doing after hip surgery," said Elsie, adjusting her glasses. "He enjoys my home cooking, but I hope he doesn't get too used to staying at home. He's been betting on online sports too ... not that he can afford it. The isolation is killing him more than anything."

"Yeah, I can understand the boredom," said Detective Harris. "So can Braylen, isn't that right? That's why he's always meddling in my case work."

"Oh ... well, I hope you get it all sorted out," said Elsie.

Braylen muttered under his breath. He remembered Harris's trial and subsequent acquittal for shooting a suspected murderer, which had flooded the news for weeks on end. Tarnishing his spot-free record, he was suspended for a couple of months and left with a bitter taste for his profession.

Detective Harris led Braylen to the enclosed interrogation area right past the lobby. "This way, asshole. We'll use the second room on the left," Detective Harris said as he opened the buzzing door. He waved Braylen through, ushering him into the interrogation room. The room was about the size of a jail cell, containing one reinforced window that you couldn't see through.

"Take a seat and tell me exactly what happened and what the hell you know about the T-bot killer." Detective Harris stood over the small gray table as Braylen sat in the hard gunmetal chair.

"Should I have my lawyer present," said Braylen dryly.

"Braylen, don't be a little bitch. Just play ball, and we'll catch a killer," said Harris. "Help us out, and you'll get some credit when it's due."

"Yeah sure, or get shot in the back," Braylen said with a smirk.

"How about worse than that. There's no cameras in this room," said Harris, giving Braylen an intense stare. "We can start taking fingers first, then work down to your tiny pecker."

"Whoa there, Detective. Is this how you treat an eyewitness and hero?" Braylen smiled. "I'm going to save your career by catching this maniac. Give me some respect. Just a little bit."

"Spill your guts and stop wasting my damn time."

"Jesus, Harris. Calm down. I was at the Cyberbar, just doing my job. I made my way to Blue's room to look for any evidence that was overlooked. As I was leaving, the killer kicked the door into my face and attacked me, pulling out a huge needle and a marine knife. The bouncer came to help, but the killer stabbed him in the chest, and I chased that bot thing until the car smashed it."

"Braylen, you're my fucking hero."

"Thanks, Harris."

"Or you're a sack of shit who got that bouncer killed with your reckless behavior." Harris heaved a big sigh and continued. "My profile of this devil-man states that he hates Tetherbots to the extreme. He targets working girls with technologically advanced capabilities, so he most likely works in tech. Him killing the user via their headset … it's unprecedented."

Braylen sat at the table, tapping his left foot on the floor. He reached into his coat pocket and set the needle weapon on the table. It was small and compact, like a ballpoint pen with an extremely sharp hypodermic needle tucked into one end. "I saved this from the self-destructing Tetherbot. It's his main weapon. This thing stuns you and fries the user's brain, too," he said, spinning the needle around.

"Forensics is checking out the T-bot. We loaded up what was left of it. Maybe it will yield some clues to our perp's identity," said Detective Harris. "I'll have them check out this needle-weapon too. Whoever made this has resources and education that should make them stand out from the crowd."

"We need to move faster. This killer is active, and now I've pissed him off," said Braylen.

"Get over yourself, Braylen. I'm the lead detective here, not you. We're moving as fast as we can, tracking video feeds all over town. We'll catch this guy soon. So, thanks for your help, but get the hell out of my way … or you'll be permanently out of the way."

"If that means I'm free to go …" Braylen leaned on the table with both arms.

"Yeah. I'm not charging you, so get the hell out," said Detective Harris, "And if you have any more information, I strongly urge you to share it with me so we can save lives."

Braylen got up from the chair and made a swift exit out the door. He was rushing through the lobby when his phone began to vibrate in his pocket. He didn't recognize the number, but he answered anyway, "Hello? Yeah, it's Braylen … okay, okay. Slow down. Where are you?

He paused, listening intently to the frantic voice on the other end. He never would have expected a call from Lynx but here she was, in danger and needed his help. "Stay where you're at and share your location. I'll meet you there." Braylen hung up, pressing the blue and white icon for Realcab, the cab company that was a rival to *Blueship*. Realcab had real human drivers, who could and would travel out-of-bounds to stay ahead of their A.I. competition.

*

Within minutes, the Realcab lowered from the heavens and hovered a few feet above the city street, waiting for Braylen to climb into the opening door. After he sat in the back seat, the door automatically closed, and the Realcab lifted into the blistering hot city skyline. The lights of the metropolis waited in anticipation for night to come.

"Take me to the City Side Apartments. I'll reward you for speed," said Braylen, handing the driver an extra ten dollars.

"Okay, mister. Buckle up. This might get a little wild," said the driver. The Realcab picked up speed, weaving through the traffic and gaining altitude, flying above the skyscrapers to make it a much faster trip. Braylen appreciated the speed, but he was still scared shitless, white knuckling his armrest the entire ride.

After what felt like a jolting rollercoaster ride without a seatbelt, the Realcab swooped down and hovered in front of Lynx's apartments. Braylen exited and thanked the driver, still a little shaken by the flight. He approached the apartments and was greeted by Lynx, who was standing on the third-floor terrace outside of her apartment door.

*

"Braylen! It's me, Sapphire … uh, I mean Lynx," Lynx shouted down the balcony, surprised by the sharp, piercing sound of her voice. The heat blazed down, temporarily blinding her. She put her arm up to block the rays. A bead of sweat rolled down between her breasts, reminding her how much she missed Sapphire. Sapphire the indestructible … Lynx the hot mess.

"What's going on? Are you okay?" Braylen shouted.

"Just a second. I'll come down."

Lynx worked her way down the stairs in a frantic rush, carrying her weekender travel bag and a large handbag. She emerged, dressed in a colorful, yet juvenile Kawaii Street fashion, including a lace trim shirt and an anime overall dress. The look was layered with a baggy, purple sleeve cardigan.

Lynx looked around the congested street uncomfortably, breathing heavily. "Let's go to the Corner Diner. I'm scared that Robert may return here," she said in a hushed voice.

"Okay. You lead the way," Braylen said, his eyebrows drawn together.

Lynx walked ahead of Braylen as she led the way to the Corner Diner. It was just two blocks down, and they made it there quickly and quietly.

"After you," Braylen said, opening the door for Lynx.

"Thank you." Lynx walked past Braylen, sitting down in a red leather-lined booth by the front windows. A neon *OPEN* sign hummed in her ear.

Braylen joined Lynx, sitting across the table from her. The diner had six other customers sprinkled throughout the space—a few at tables and a couple of stragglers on counter stools.

"What can I get for you two?" A perky robotic waitress with the nametag "Alice" stood over them dressed in classic 1950s attire. From her chest down to her pelvis, were shelves full of warm food, lit up under infrared heating lamps. She also had chilled food, milk products, and creamers.

"We'll have some coffee, black please," Lynx said, smiling back at Alice's exaggeratedly clownish grin.

Braylen nodded his head in agreement.

Alice walked back behind the counter, grabbed mugs, and poured the coffees. Three fresh plates were set under a heat lamp as a cook rang a bell and shouted, "Order up!"

Alice dropped off two coffees to Lynx and Braylen and returned to get the plates of warm food for her cache.

"So, what's the emergency?" asked Braylen, grabbing his coffee and taking a sip.

"I was just attacked by the killer. Well, not me, but Sapphire. And you know what? Robert ... Robert did it. He has her, and I think he's coming for me. My best friend, Robert Chaise, is the murderer." Lynx started choking up, trying to hold back tears.

"What? How do you know it's this Robert guy? Did you see him?" Braylen looked skeptical, as if he doubted the credibility of the nineteen-year-old.

"No, but I recognized his voice when he talked to me. Even with the distorted voice, I know it's him."

Braylen studied Lynx before replying. "I have to call Detective Harris so they can search his place." Braylen pulled out his phone and called the precinct. His phone was ringing for a while before reaching the automated dispatch when a loud *BANG* rang out through the diner.

The customers were sent scrambling, screaming, and ducking for cover as Sapphire walked out from the kitchen carrying a smoking shotgun. She was still wearing her outfit from earlier, even the dildo. The cook's mangled body lay on the floor in a growing pool of scarlet red.

"Sapphire?! No! How is this happening?" Lynx blinked wildly.

"Get down! She's going to kill you!" Braylen shouted. He flipped the table on its side, sending their coffees crashing to the floor along with a napkin bin and condiments. He crouched down behind the table with Lynx joining him.

Another loud *BANG* echoed through the diner as Sapphire fired another shell. Alice dropped to the ceramic-tiled floor. Her robotic head slammed down, and sparks erupted instantly from her damaged skull. The serving tray of food intermixed with robotic parts, coagulating milk products with Alice's fluids on the floor.

Three customers raced for the door. Broken glass and coffee puddles crunched and splashed under their feet as they pushed open the front door and scrambled outside. Another blast followed them, crashing through the glass, and hitting one of the customers in the back, knocking them to the cement ground in front of the cars parked in the parking lot. Another customer was cowering behind a table in the corner.

Sapphire turned her attention back to Lynx and Braylen, firing a shot into the table and splintering the wood into Swiss cheese.

Braylen knew they had to act quickly … one more shot to the table would completely obliterate it. He slowly pulled the needle weapon from his coat pocket. Before he left the interrogation room, he had swapped it with a pen he had in his pocket, leaving Detective Harris with a simple writing utensil. Sapphire racked the shotgun, getting ready for another blast.

"Robert! Stop this! I know you're in there. You don't have to keep killing," Lynx shouted in anguish from behind the table. "You're not like this! You're a good person."

"It's the ultimate irony. Something that gave you pleasure is now going to give you the worst pain," Sapphire said in her sultry voice. "But it's too late now for you and for whoever tries to stop me."

Braylen was shaking and scared shitless, but he steadied the needle in his hand and found the button on the side that would activate it. He looked over at Lynx, who was shaking and crying, but trying to hold it together. "Keep her talking so I can get a clear shot at her," he whispered.

"Sapphire, you're misbehaving. You were made for love, not killing," Lynx said, trying to distract Robert. "I'm sorry I didn't listen before. I'm sorry. Just . . . let's just put the gun down and get back to normal."

"There is no normal … not until all the Tetherbots have been destroyed and all the puppeteers have been freed," Robert yelled as Sapphire. "Ready to be freed?" Sapphire fired another shot—the shotgun shell ripped through the table.

Shell fragments splintered off, striking Lynx at the top of her shoulder. Blood splattered behind her, spraying onto the white floor behind her. "Ahhhh," Lynx screamed as the searing pain burned through her body.

Braylen sprang up from behind the crumbling table as if in slow motion. Lining up a precise shot with the needle, he pressed the button and it stretched out toward Sapphire's neck. The hypodermic needle plunged into her, paralyzing Sapphire before she could take another step.

"I've got you now, you coward!" Braylen shouted as he held the needle in position. He looked over to Lynx, shouting. "Lynx! How bad are you?"

"It's looking pretty bad," said the one remaining customer, who had inched forward to tend to Lynx's wound. "I'm a nurse," he said, applying pressure to the punctures with a towel.

"Fry him, Braylen. Fry him," Lynx pleaded. "Press the button to fry Robert, before he has the chance to remove the headset."

Braylen looked down at the weapon, but only saw the one button that he had used to extend the needle. "How do I do that?" he asked. But Lynx was unresponsive. She had passed out with her back leaning against the booth seat, head tilted to the side.

"The cops and paramedics are on the way," someone yelled from outside the diner.

Braylen held the button down, praying that the needle weapon would work. After about five seconds, a jolt of electricity surged through the needle into Sapphire's neck, burning her circuits and sending her and the shotgun jolting to the ground. Her android body shook and convulsed until she finally seized into a statuesque figure. Her arm was sticking straight up into the air, her legs were stuck in a scissor position.

"I did it! I did it, Lynx!" shouted Braylen. He looked around for confirmation, hardly believing it himself.

Loud sirens blared in the distance, getting closer and closer with each second. Police cars came pouring into the parking lot from the street and from the air. Paramedics arrived among the chaos and rushed to help the wounded. Detective Harris was one of the first officers to get inside and assess the damage.

He charged in, his face red with anger. "Braylen, what the fuck happened over here?"

"We stopped our killer. That's what happened," said Braylen.

"It's complete chaos in here! And I don't see the killer … just some T-bot. So what's the story, Braylen?" Detective Harris prodded.

"The killer's name is Robert Chaise. He used an innocent woman's Tetherbot to try to kill her. We need to find him, Harris. He might have died when I activated his needle weapon."

"Okay, everyone. We're locking this place down!" Detective Harris barked. "This is an active crime scene. I want interviews and forensics conducted ASAP!"

The police officers went to work, sectioning off the diner with yellow police tape, working with rubber gloves on their hands. Two other officers held back the reporters and onlookers from the neighborhood as the paramedics removed the victims on stretchers. The forensic team began collecting and bagging the shotgun, shells, and robotic parts.

"Braylen, you're coming with me. Get in my car, now!" Detective Harris said as he walked out of the diner.

"Yeah? Now you need me?" Braylen called back. "I thought you wanted me to get out of your way," he said. He shrugged and followed Detective Harris out the door.

Chapter 10

The Hunt

Detective Harris and Braylen landed at Robert Chaise's house, nearly jumping out of the unmarked black Skyflyer. The house was dark inside; a loose gutter banging against the decorative red brickwork with each gust of wind. A circular bay window ominously overlooked the front yard, highlighting the attic. Detective Harris led the way to the battered house with Braylen lagging close behind. A motion-sensor light popped on as they approached, illuminating the dirty, overgrown cement walkway as they approached the front door.

"Stay back, Braylen. Let me go first … just in case we encounter someone," said Detective Harris. He pulled out his gun from the holster and switched off the safety.

"Okay, lead the way. I'll watch your back," said Braylen.

Detective Harris opened the screen door and turned the door handle. It was locked.

"We could call in SWAT to bash it down," Braylen suggested.

Detective Harris paused to think. "I'll call it in. Let's check around back in the meantime," said Detective Harris. He pushed a few buttons on his smartwatch, keeping his voice low and steady as he talked into it. "Yeah, Detective Harris here. I'm going to need a breach team. Send one to my current location."

They walked around a cement path that led to the fenced backyard. Detective Harris opened a latch and swung the wooden gate open. The hinges squealed in protest as it moved, and the partially rotted wood wobbled in places as it fully opened. The long grass and wildflowers revealed the lack of maintenance, but it was quiet, with no sign of any dogs or animal life. As Braylen and Harris walked slowly together, another motion-detecting light beamed to life, lighting up a small portion of the backyard. Insects swarmed to the lights, bouncing around in a flurry.

"Look, there's a sliding glass door on the deck. I can bust the glass or pop it off the track," Braylen said as they trudged through the rough grass.

"I got this." Detective Harris hopped up the steps. The weakening wood bent and bowed under each step.

"Watch it. That wood is rotten," Braylen warned.

Detective Harris walked to the sliding door as the rotting deck held up under the pressure. He looked inside, but it was so dark, he could only make out a few shapes in the living room. "Doesn't look like anyone's home," he said, peering into the room.

"He's here, I know it. We have to get inside and get him. The needle weapon should have shocked him into a vegetative state," Braylen said. He picked up a piece of broken concrete from the crumbling walkway and handed it to Detective Harris.

"That should work. Stand back." Harris held the concrete piece in his right hand and stepped back, getting into a right-handed throwing stance. "Okay. As soon as I break this, I'll head in first. Gun out."

Braylen nodded in agreement, and Detective Harris tossed the chunk of concrete into the left side of the sliding glass doors. The glass imploded into a pile of jagged transparent shards, echoing throughout the neighborhood.

Quiet returned quickly like a morgue after a wake. You could hear a pin drop in the darkness. Then, the crunching of glass under their feet broke the mundane silence as Detective Harris proceeded with extreme caution toward a light coming from under a door—the only light visible in the dark domain. "Over here. There's a light on. Watch my back when I open it." Detective Harris walked over to the door, bumping into a living room couch with his hip.

"Okay, open it. I'm ready," said Braylen, standing behind Detective Harris. Braylen had his dad's old police gun strapped to his hip. It was his back-up piece, which he only used in special cases. He drew the gun and readied it for use, waiting for the door to open with a nervousness he'd seldom experienced.

After a brief pause that felt like forever, Detective Harris opened the door, revealing a stairway down to the basement. A lone light bulb above his head lit the way down to a dark, dirty dungeon with what appeared to be soiled cobblestone. Cobwebs and inches of dust covered everything.

"Police! If anyone is here, make yourself known," shouted Detective Harris.

"Clean up this shithole, Geaves," Braylen said.

"Just watch my back, and cut the chatter," Detective Harris said, stepping down the last few steps to the basement's dirt-covered linoleum floor.

Detective Harris raised his gun, finger on the trigger as he walked slowly forward. In front of him were rows of boxes about waist-high overflowing with robotic limbs, arms and heads. The boxes lined the hallway forming a narrow hoarder's path, and they followed it until they reached a large, carpeted room. The room was remodeled with fresh paint and furnished as a living room, swallowing up a lonely couch and a television set. Newspapers were strewn about the floor— some about Tetherbots, but most about the serial killer. Next to the newspapers lay one book called *Your Tetherbot, Now What?*

Sitting on the couch was the Tetherbot named Audry. Her radiant red hair was draped over her vacant face, while the light from the T.V. danced across her doe-like eyes. She was completely naked, and her large breasts garnered Detective Harris's attention as he entered the room. He lowered his weapon and tried to conceal his embarrassment.

"Um, excuse me, Miss. Are you alone in the house?" said Detective Harris.

There was no response. She sat there expressionless, staring at the T.V. with a blank face, her eyes glossed over under a blanket of long, wispy lashes. Her eyes didn't blink, and her body didn't move. She didn't even breathe as they inched closer.

"Tetherbot …" Braylen announced as he stepped in behind Harris.

"Yeah, I noticed. Thanks for your expertise."

"Over in the corner. Look, there's a light coming from under the floor," Braylen said, pointing to the light seeping out from under the wall.

"Looks like a hidden room. How do we open it?" Detective Harris walked over to the wall in question and slid his hand across the smooth vinyl wood paneling, not finding anything abnormal.

"There's got to be a hidden switch or device to activate it. Look around. Check the shelves," Detective Harris surmised.

Braylen checked a tan wooden bookshelf that was behind the couch against the wall. It was filled from top to bottom with books, mostly technology and mathematics books, sprinkled in with some philosophy and history books. Braylen scanned through them, looking to see if any of the books were odd or out of place. He ran his fingers under the shelves for switches or buttons, but only came up with thick layers of dust on his hands. "I'm not finding anything over here … just books and dust," he said.

"Pull the damn books off the shelves. Put some effort in it. It's got to be somewhere."

Braylen started at the top and knocked a row of books to the floor, causing a haze of dust and dirt. "Great. What the fuck did that do except fill my lungs with fucking shit," Braylen protested.

"Okay. Get the next row," said Detective Harris. He reached up to the top of the door, searching for a key on the frame.

Braylen grabbed the bookshelf and tipped it over, dumping all the books to the floor in a cascading plume of cough-inducing irritants.

"Great job. Now you fucked it up. Here. Lift it up with me," said Detective Harris.

Braylen grabbed one side of the bookshelf, Detective Harris the other. Together, they pushed it back up against the wall. The pile of books slid around on the floor and came to a rest in a mound of torn pages and hard covers.

"Ha, I knew it! Look!" Detective Harris said. He pointed to a book sitting on the middle shelf. "Pull it forward. That should open the door. But be ready … the motherfucker is probably right behind this wall."

Braylen pulled the book forward. As Harris had predicted, the wall door opened, gliding quickly across some rails, revealing a high-tech VR room. The room was black with soundproof, acoustic foam lining the walls. Flat panel screens were strategically placed in the corners, tilting down at a forty-five-degree angle toward the center of the room. Attached to a harness and hooked up to a VR headset was a hunched over Robert, eerily lifeless and slowly swinging back and forth.

"I think he's dead, or at least brain dead," Braylen observed, inching closer to Robert.

"Don't touch him or do anything else," Detective Harris commanded. "This is a crime scene. I'm going to lock it down. My team will be here in a few more minutes."

Bam! The lights above them popped in a dramatic fashion, shrouding them in complete darkness. The men strained their eyes in the dark, extending their arms in front of them to feel around for their surroundings.

"Fuck! How the hell did that happen?" Braylen shouted.

As if to answer, there was a determined clattering noise coming from the left side of the room. "What the …?" Braylen caught a glimpse of a shadowy figure, coming right at him.

Detective Harris activated the flashlight on his wristwatch and lit up the area, exposing Vannoy, who was a few feet from Braylen. She was wearing a cut-off T-shirt and Daisy Duke jorts. She looked wild with her blonde hair flowing down her shoulders and blue eyes ablaze in the dim light. Vannoy had a whip in her right hand; she cracked it at Braylen, slicing his hand.

"Ah, you bitch!" Braylen yelped, dropping his gun on the dark floor. He reached down with his bloodied hand to pick it up but was thwarted when another crack of the whip pushed the gun out of his reach.

With his wrists crossed over so the light shined over his gun, Detective Harris aimed at Vannoy. He fired a round and as the muzzle flash lit up the room, smoke filled the air. The bullet hit Vannoy landing in the left side of the shoulder, sending her staggering to the right—but she held on firmly to the whip in a death grip, refusing to let go. The small bullet hole revealed circuits and wires, while a blue milky fluid started seeping out of her shoulder.

"Another damn Tetherbot! For a guy who hates them, he sure owns a few," Braylen shouted. "Watch out!"

During the blackout, Audry had snuck up behind Detective Harris. She smashed a wooden dining chair over his back, breaking the chair and knocking him down to the floor in a heap, his gun bouncing across the floor.

"Harris! You damn bots are going to pay," Braylen said, rushing Audry like a linebacker. The crack of Vannoy's whip followed Braylen, hitting him square on the ass. It tore his pants, but he was unstoppable. In seconds, he lowered a shoulder and tackled her, lifting her up and slamming her into the ground. Audry's head popped off like a mannequin, rolling into the padded wall. Sparks and fluids followed every turn of the head.

Vannoy cracked her whip again, slicing Braylen's cheek wide open. Blood slung up into the air as he screamed in pain, but there was no time to stop and assess the damage. Braylen knew he had to move, and fast. Guided by the light from Harris' watch, Braylen threw himself across the floor, grabbed his gun, turned on his side, and fired two shots at Vannoy. Braylen watched the first bullet rip through Vannoy's ear and penetrate the soundproof wall behind her. The second bullet hit her chin with a loud *TINK*, splitting her mouth open and breaking her front teeth; the teeth rattled onto the floor like loose change falling to the ground. Her eyes looked down at Braylen with intent to kill as if she was unaware of the missing ear or teeth. Braylen steadied himself, watching Vannoy carefully.

Vannoy stumbled to the right, her missing ear revealing complex wiring within her synthetic skull. She spun toward Braylen and cracked the whip at him, slapping the gun from his hand again. The gun went off with a bang as it hit the floor, sending a round off into the semi-darkness. Simultaneously, Vannoy rushed Braylen, scratching and clawing at him in a wild fury. Her nails dug into Braylen's arms as he held them up to block her onslaught. He kicked her back with both feet and enough force to send her stumbling into the padded wall.

Vannoy regained balance and began walking toward Braylen with murderous vengeance, ready to pounce on him like a cat finishing off a mouse. She threw a kick at the crouching man, hitting him in the side of the head and knocking him onto his stomach. She dropped to her knees, grabbed Braylen by the back of his hair, and pulled his face up.

"Robert will get his revenge," Vannoy slurred out of her broken mouth.

Suddenly, a loud crash was heard, and the breach team smashed through the wall with a battering ram, sending wood splinters everywhere. The first team member opened fire on Vannoy, striking her repeatedly in the forehead and dropping her instantly.

"Good God. It's about damn time," said Braylen. He looked up as if he had just witnessed a miracle.

"Is this Harris?" asked an officer, dropping to his knees to attend to the limp body.

"Yeah, who else would it be? And don't worry about me, I'm fine," said Braylen sarcastically. He slowly rose to his knees, steadying himself with his hand on the way up. Blood was streaming down his cheek, and he used his sleeve to blot at it.

"Robert is in the harness. Take him into the ambulance with extreme caution. Make sure he's strapped down," Braylen instructed. "Get Harris into a stretcher. Jesus Christ, move it, folks."

EMT personnel rushed in moments later, wheeling in their stretchers and equipment. Braylen watched them unstrap Robert and load him up, followed by Harris.

Wrong order thought Braylen, realizing he could have been kinder to Harris. They may have had their differences, but he sincerely hoped Detective Harris was alright.

Chapter 11
The Aftermath

Life was good without a serial killer on the loose. Robert was in the hospital, chained to his bed in a vegetative state, and Lynx was back home, safe in her apartment. Everyone at the Cyberbar was super supportive, especially Hazza, who started Sapphire a Funder account with a weekly payout. For the time being, Lynx was recovering at home with the promise to return to work as Sapphire within a month's time, which was more than enough time for Lynx to heal.

There was a knock at the door.

Then another knock.

Then another, louder knock.

Fear and anxiety hit Lynx like a ton of bricks. The feeling that someone was out to get her returned as she summoned the courage to look through the peephole. To her relief, the techs from Tetherbot were at her door (complete in their black haptic suits) with a two-wheeled utility cart carrying a big, black crate. Lynx excitedly opened the door.

"She's all ready to go. I made all the necessary repairs myself," said the first Tetherbot tech proudly. He had a big forehead and a bulbous nose above a thick mustache—like a handsome version of Groucho Marx.

"I still can't believe she made it through all she did. I'd never seen anything like this Tetherbot. She's one tough bot," said the other Tetherbot tech, still scratching his head. He whimsically whisked his multi-colored hair back in a wave.

"Where would you like her?" said Groucho.

"Just drop her in front of the couch please," said Lynx, swallowing in a dry throat.

The techs wheeled in the crate and set it down, quickly unstrapping it from the cart and sliding the cart out. After Lynx signed the release form, the techs headed out the door as quickly as they came in. Lynx unbolted the easy release clasps and opened the lid, staring at the contents inside.

There was Sapphire in all her glory.

Lynx moved Sapphire to the couch, cradling her like a baby. "Look at you. I thought I lost you. But you're invincible. You don't miss a beat, do you? It's hardly fair to the others. You and I ... we were unstoppable. But I'm warning you, Sapphire ... if I turn you back on, you can't expect to take over my life. That, I won't allow."

Sapphire stared blank-eyed in blissful unawareness.

"Must be nice to shut off like that. You and I aren't so different there," said Lynx. She found herself unconsciously zipping up her haptic suit. She hadn't even realized she was slipping it on. "I guess this is the moment of truth. Are you ready?" She took a deep breath in, then out, expanding her diaphragm as she did so.

"Let's give it a whirl." Lynx's heart palpitated rapidly as she picked up the VR headset and slipped it over her head gracefully. She touched the power button, awaiting the familiar Tetherbot home screen, but it never arrived. Instead, she was greeted by a few command codes on a black screen, a moment of static, and then finally the blue Tetherbot home screen. She figured this was a normal part of the reboot process.

Finally, Sapphire powered back to life, and Lynx took control of her hands as she glanced at them in amazement. It felt bittersweet to be back inside the safety net of Sapphire's robotic cocoon.

Without warning, Sapphire walked to the kitchen, unscripted, as if hypnotized.

"Hey, don't go that way," Lynx commanded. Lynx tried to regain control, stomping her feet on the ground. "STOP," bellowed both voices, overlapping.

Sapphire grabbed a large kitchen knife, brandishing it upwards in her hand like a mechanical killer. "POWER OFF!" Lynx desperately pushed all the buttons she could, holding the power button down again, but nothing happened.

Sapphire started her murderous course toward Lynx like a cancerous inertia. Lynx yanked the VR headset off her head and threw it across the room.

"STOP! What are you doing?" shouted Lynx, holding the power button down. "STOP, I said!" Lynx began to cry, backing up past the couch and into the hallway.

Sapphire continued forward, waving the knife, which was shining in the air. Then suddenly, she stopped to admire her reflection in the shiny knife. Her lips parted in a devious smile before she finally said, "Robert says 'Hi'."

THE END

ACKNOWLEDGMENTS

Big thanks to our editor, Marissa Taylor, who has been there for us since day one. Thank you for your critical eye. Your industry experience is an essential ingredient to our success.

Huge thanks to Bookfly Designs for designing such a wicked cover design. You took our vision and exceeded our expectations. Working with you was as easy as breathing.

We are also indebted to Detective Darrehshoori for providing invaluable information regarding police procedures and protocols. You came into our lives and saved the day at the eleventh hour, like the true crime-fighting hero that you are.

Thanks to our writing friends on Facebook in Write About Now, including authors, Ryan Rutan, Riley Cross, and Matt Micheli. Riley, I thank the day I met you. Also—read her book.

Geoffrey A. Jourden: Thank you to Raija, Giovanni, and Taimi for being supportive while I typed away. I love you all so much.

T.M. Rivera: Clementina Rivera, you are my guardian angel, best friend, and life force. I love you endlessly. Jacob Garcia, thank you for all your loving support. Thank you to all my supportive friends, including Ryan Rutan, Robert Robertson, Randal Patches, Chris R., and Armando Marroquin. Ryan wrote this awesome book, Fork This Life, which inspired us to keep trucking. Robert, thank you for always looking out for me and my family. Armando, thanks for encouraging me to stay loyal to my craft. You were my first book buddy. Thank you, Chris R., long-time, true-blue friend. Randal, you've been a gem of a friend since the good old college days. Thank you to Crystal G. and Jahzeel C. Crystal, thank you for cheering me on to follow my dreams. And Jahzeel, you have rooted me on from day one.